Bring Back
Yesterday

books by harriet sirof

Because She's My Friend

Bring Back Yesterday

Bring Back
Yesterday

harriet sirof

• A Jean Karl Boook •

ATHENEUM BOOKS FOR YOUNG READERS

Atheneum Books for Young Readers
An imprint of Simon & Schuster Children's Publishing Division
1230 Avenue of the Americas
New York, New York 10020

Book design by Anne Scatto / PIXEL PRESS

The text of this book is set in Monotype Walbaum.

First Edition

Printed in the United States of America

10 9 8 7 6 5 4 3 2 1

Library of Congress Cataloging-in-Publication Data
Sirof, Harriet.
Bring back yesterday / Harriet Sirof. — 1st ed.
p. cm.
"A Jean Karl book."
Summary: When her parents die in a plane crash, thirteen-year-old Lisa
escapes from her grief and her new life with her aunt through
returning to the past and an imaginary playmate.
ISBN 0-689-80638-8
[1. Death—Fiction. 2. Grief—Fiction. 3. Aunts—Fiction.
4. Imaginary playmates—Fiction.] I. Title.
PZ7.S6217Br   1996
[Fic]—dc20
95-36722

For Jason, Keith, and Olivia

Bring Back Yesterday

chapter
1

When I was little, I had an imaginary friend named Rooji. Sometimes Rooji was a boy and other times she was a girl. Sometimes she was as big as a lion and other times he was small enough to hide in my pocket. That made perfect sense to me. Wasn't I the same person in my favorite yellow overalls with the bunny patches on the knees as when Mommy dressed me up in the pink pinafore that Grandma sent from Arizona for my birthday?

My mother didn't like Rooji. When we put away my toys for the night, she always said, "A place for everything and everything in its place." Rooji didn't have a proper place or size or anything. That was almost worse than being imaginary.

I couldn't understand why it upset my mother that she couldn't see Rooji. It didn't bother her that Grandma was only a voice on the telephone and you couldn't see what she looked like. I always knew exactly what Rooji looked like because I made pictures of him on the back of my eyelids. And Rooji was always there when I needed her.

At night, my parents would leave my bedroom door open a crack so they could hear me if I woke up and cried. That meant Rooji and I could hear them talking in the living room. We would scrunch down under the covers and listen.

My mother would say, "I thought it would stop when she started nursery school." I knew "it" was Rooji and "she" was me.

My father would say, "You're making a mountain out of a molehill."

I knew what mountains were. They were where you went for summer vacation. And a mole was that ugly brown thing the old lady down the hall had on her face. But what was a molehill?

Once my mother said, "Her teacher says that Lisa is a sweet, well-behaved child who follows directions well. The problem is that she really doesn't relate to the other children."

Rooji poked me. "You're scared of the other kids."

"I am not."

"You are, too."

I hissed, "Shut up!" even though my mother didn't like me to talk like the kids at school. She wanted me to be friends with them without being like them.

My father said, "She has only been in nursery school for a few weeks. Give her time to adjust."

My mother said, "Her teacher told me that when the class plays games, Lisa hangs back whispering to herself. We know who she is whispering to."

My father said, "She is just going through a stage. She will make friends in school and forget all about that imaginary what's-its-name."

"I won't!" I said almost loud enough for them to hear. I told Rooji, "I hate the kids in school. They pick on me. They call me Cry-baby when I tell the teacher like Mommy said I should if I wasn't happy."

Rooji said, "They're doo-doos."

I would never call anyone a doo-doo. I was a good girl and that was a bad word. But I giggled when Rooji said it.

My giggle encouraged Rooji. She declared, "Big, fat, smelly doo-doo heads."

I laughed so hard that I had to stuff a corner of my blanket into my mouth to keep my parents from hearing. Then, before Rooji could make me laugh again, I said, "Let's play Eensy Weensy Spider."

We sang, "The eensy weensy spider went up the water spout..."

☙❧

My father had predicted that I would make friends and forget all about Rooji. He turned out to be half right. Although I never got the knack of attracting friends, I did finally forget Rooji. It just took longer than Dad expected.

It took me a long time to give up the security of always having someone at my side who was on my side. My parents loved me and did what was best for me, but I felt... It's hard to describe what I felt. Sort of that they were so big and I was so small. They knew everything. They could do everything. They never made mistakes. And their words made things happen. My words didn't have any power. But Rooji listened to me anyway. Besides, two against one isn't fair. Rooji evened things up.

Rooji and I stayed best friends until after I started elementary school. My father got me into his school (not the school the other kids on the block went to) so he and my mother could choose my teachers and watch my progress. I had to call them Mr. and Mrs. Barnett in school because Dad was the assistant principal and Mom was the reading teacher. And they expected me to make them proud of me.

I did. I got all *Excellent*s on my report cards.

It was lucky Rooji didn't get a report card. Rooji wouldn't sit still in her seat. She wouldn't pay attention to the lessons. She sang silly songs in my ear during arithmetic and dropped my pencils on the floor while I was copying the spelling words. Rooji didn't care that we had to set a good example.

Scolding her didn't do any good. Finally, when she started flipping the pages of my book during free reading time, I told her if she was so bored with school she should wait for me at home.

I loved to read. Wonderful worlds were waiting for me in

the pages of books. While I was deep in a book, I could pretend that it was all happening to me. I was always begging my mother to let me stay up to finish reading the chapter. When I finally had to turn my light out, I'd act out the book under the covers with myself as the hero.

At first I gave Rooji important roles in my nighttime plays. She was the Bad Hat to my Madeline, Pooh to my Christopher Robin, the white rabbit to my Alice. But she kept making the stories come out different, even though I told her you couldn't change what was written in a book. So I gave her smaller and smaller parts.

Rooji didn't complain. She just started wandering off while I was busy with my play. Often she didn't come back until after I'd fallen asleep. Gradually, she stayed away longer and longer. For days at a time. Then weeks.

I didn't notice when Rooji finally disappeared altogether. As the months and years passed, I forgot that she had ever existed. I forgot that I had once had an imaginary friend to keep me company and comfort me.

I forgot all about Rooji until a few days after the plane crash.

chapter

2

Dates in history are labeled B.C. or A.D.: before or after the birth of Christ. My life should be dated B.P.C. and A.P.C.: before and after the plane crash. Before, my life was quiet and orderly. I went to school Monday through Friday. I liked school and got good grades. I usually ate lunch with Jill, who sang in the school chorus with me, and some of her friends. Chorus practice was Tuesdays after class. Other afternoons I jogged if the weather was good and then did my homework until dinnertime. Mom, Dad, and I discussed the day's events over dinner. Then I studied, read, or watched TV. Sometimes Jill and I studied for tests together. Sunday morning was my jazz exercise class, and Sunday evenings I ate out with my parents. My parents took me to a Broadway show four times a year: once for each of our birthdays and once for Mom and Dad's anniversary. I loved going to the theater.

Then Mom and Dad were invited to speak about their school's reading program at an educational conference in London, and my life was changed forever. Although the invitation was a great honor, Mom said she couldn't go. She couldn't leave me for four days. And it didn't make sense to pay all that airfare and have me miss school to sit alone in a hotel room while she and Dad were busy with the conference. She urged Dad to go by himself. Dad said Mom had contributed as much as he had to the reading program. He refused to go without her.

I insisted I'd be fine on my own. They wouldn't leave until Wednesday evening. I had school on Thursday and Friday. Saturday, I'd call Jill and we'd work on our English reports together. We were reading *A Midsummer Night's Dream* in school, and our English teacher had assigned us reports on Shakespeare's England. I was writing my report on the theaters; Jill was writing about the courts. It would be Sunday before I knew it, with exercise class in the morning and Mom and Dad coming home in the evening.

Mom said she wished I had a good friend I could stay with. In the end, after much soul-searching and discussion, my parents flew to London—leaving me alone for the first time in my life.

Not completely alone. There was a list of emergency phone numbers on the refrigerator. Mom arranged for our weekly cleaning woman to come in an extra day and for our neighbors down the hall, Mrs. Winkler and Mrs. Seeley, to give me dinner on the evenings she'd be gone. Besides which, I was to call Aunt Alice every night to report that I was all right.

I didn't mind the dinners. Mom worried about Dad's cholesterol, so she mostly made fish or chicken with fresh fruit for dessert. I lapped up Mrs. Seeley's pot roast with mashed potatoes and gravy and Mrs. Winkler's chocolate cheesecake. I didn't mind making polite conversation while I stuffed my face. When I asked Mrs. Seeley about her new grandchild, she was good for the whole dinner. And once I got Mrs. Winkler started on Russian Jews I could tune out and gorge myself. Talking to Aunt Alice was a lot harder.

Aunt Alice was Mom's younger sister (a lot younger). She was our only relative besides Grandma (Dad's mother) in Arizona. We lived in Manhattan, and Aunt Alice lived across the bridge in Brooklyn. It was probably only about twenty minutes away by subway, but somehow we never went to visit her. Aunt Alice came to visit us a few times a year. The last time I saw her was at Thanksgiving dinner. Because she was a vegetarian, she refused to eat the turkey Mom spent all day making.

When I called Aunt Alice on Thursday night, she seemed surprised to hear from me. Like she'd forgotten that Mom had spoken to her for a half hour arranging the best time for me to check in without interrupting her office hours or anything. Her forgetting made me uncomfortable, but I was brought up to have good manners. It wasn't polite to say, "Hello. This is Lisa. I'm calling because Mom said I should. Good-bye." But she made it hard for me to spin out a five-minute conversation. When I asked how her cat was, the answer was "Healthy." I was almost reduced to "Eaten any good tofu lately?" I began to understand why Mom usually sounded annoyed when she talked about her "vegetarian veterinarian sister."

If Aunt Alice didn't want manners, it wasn't up to me to force them on her. I made Friday and Saturday's calls short and sweet. And I didn't call on Sunday when Mom and Dad were due back.

I didn't go to Mrs. Seeley for dinner on Sunday either. My parents were coming home in a few hours, and I'd hardly had a chance to be on my own. I ordered a pepperoni pizza and sat on the sofa eating it while I listened to the new CDs I'd bought with the last of the money Dad had left me. I was supposed to be finishing Act 2 of *A Midsummer Night's Dream* for English, but I was enjoying the freedom to be a lazy slob.

The phone on Mom's desk rang. I picked it up, stretching out the cord so I could eat while I talked.

Aunt Alice sounded like she had a cold. She asked, "Have your parents come home yet?"

I swallowed hastily. "They'll be back in a few hours. That's why I didn't check in with you tonight. I'm sorry if I worried you."

She ignored my apology. "Do you know their flight number?"

"Sorry, no. It's the one landing at Kennedy at eight o'clock if that helps."

There was a silence. Then she said, "I think I'll come over and wait for them with you."

I rushed to clean up the evidence of my living room picnic. I gobbled the last pizza slice, threw out the box, and Dust-bustered the telltale crumbs off the sofa. Then I sat down and opened my Shakespeare book. But Aunt Alice's phone call bugged me. She hadn't taken the job of overseeing me very seriously. So why had she suddenly decided to come over? Why had she talked to me in the voice that any four-year-old knows means "Keep it from the child?"

I have a very active imagination. Last year I got a strange little lump on my wrist and I was sure it was cancer. I lay awake in bed at night planning my funeral. Of course, the cancer turned out to be a wart that the doctor removed in two minutes. Aunt Alice's call was sure to be a wart, but that didn't stop the pepperoni from churning in my stomach.

I picked up the TV remote and flipped through the channels. There was Bill Cosby selling pudding pops, the Enterprise heading for the planet Bre'el Four, a reporter describing a plane crash.

It took a long time to register. When it finally did, my mind refused to accept it. The things you see on TV don't have anything to do with you. Roseanne tells D. J. to go play in traffic, *Nature* slows the flight of a hummingbird, an earthquake levels a town in Turkestan. Touch a button on the remote and they disappear. A plane headed from London to New York crashes into a hillside. Touch a button and switch to the newest episode of *ER*.

●◦●

The doorbell and the telephone rang at the same time. I stood still, stalling, putting disaster off for a few more seconds. Then I opened the door to Aunt Alice and let her answer the phone.

The person on the other end did all the talking. Aunt Alice just growled "Yes" and "No" and "I see." Her face looked like it was made of vanilla ice cream that was melting. It wasn't hard to guess that she was hearing that Mom and Dad were on the plane that crashed.

She hung up, put her arm around me, and patted my shoulder gently. Like I might break into pieces if she patted too hard. I pulled away and shook my head. It had to be some ridiculous mistake. Soon the key would turn in the lock and Dad would come in saying that the conference had been very stimulating and Mom would ask how I'd managed without them.

Aunt Alice murmured, "I know."

I said "Excuse me" and ran into the bathroom and threw up.

The doorbell rang as I came out. Mrs. Seeley and Mrs. Winkler had seen the news on TV. They came running to make sure everything was all right. When they heard that everything was all wrong, they stayed to help. They clattered around the kitchen while Aunt Alice sat at Mom's desk making phone calls. She called Grandma in Arizona to break the news, the airline to arrange Grandma's flight to New York, and Dr. Sung, another veterinarian, to handle emergencies. Whenever she hung up for a second, the phone rang immediately: the principal and teachers from Mom and Dad's school, Mom's friend in Chicago. How did the whole world know so soon?

When I went into the kitchen for something to take the awful taste of vomit out of my mouth, I interrupted Mrs. Seeley and Mrs. Winkler's talk of the "arrangements under the circumstances." Seeing me, they immediately switched the subject, discussing what to cook for tomorrow's dinner in loud, false voices. They needn't have bothered. I didn't know or care what they were talking about. All the ringing and clattering and talking was running together into one dizzying wave of noise in my head.

Mrs. Winkler offered me things: a glass of cold milk, a cup of hot chocolate. Mrs. Seeley suggested things: a bath, a nap. I fled into the living room where I scrunched down into Dad's easy chair. I hugged my arms around my knees and squeezed my eyes shut. I went into a kind of trance—seeing nothing, hearing nothing, feeling nothing.

I sat hunched into a tight ball until my arms and legs went numb. While flexing my hands to bring the blood back into them, I noticed my watch. Was it only two hours since Aunt Alice called? Impossible. I turned on the ten o'clock news.

Aunt Alice interrupted her phone conversation to ask me, "Are you sure you want to see that?"

"I'll turn it off if it bothers you."

"I thought it might bother *you*."

"Do you want me to turn it off?"

"I want you to do whatever makes you feel better."

We'd have gone on like that all night if the person on the phone hadn't coughed to attract Aunt Alice's attention. She went back to telling Dr. Sung to check on a dog who wouldn't eat. I stared at the TV.

I had expected to see a real plane crash, a fierce explosion into fire and smoke like in a disaster movie. There was just a reporter in front of a map with a dotted line to show the plane's path and an *X* to mark the crash site. Then the picture switched to the victims' families hearing the news at the airport. Watching them, I felt I was letting Mom and Dad down. Everyone else was screaming and crying and fainting. I was sitting like a bump on a log.

The plane crash was the big thing on the news. I watched it again at eleven o'clock and all over again on *Good Morning America*. I bought the newspapers, the *Times* and the *News* in the morning and the *Post* in the afternoon, and read every word. By the morning, everyone knew that the plane hadn't just crashed. It had been blown up by a terrorist bomb. The terrorists had called the news media to boast that the bombing was a victory for their cause. What did terrorists from a country I'd never heard of and a cause I didn't understand have to do with Mom and Dad? What did they have to do with me?

●━●

Nothing seemed to have anything to do with me. Grandma came and settled into Mom and Dad's room. Aunt Alice ran home for a sleeping bag to bunk down on the living room floor. People started paying sympathy calls. They trooped through the apartment introducing themselves as teachers from Mom and Dad's school or members of the organizations they'd belonged to. Everyone said it was so terrible, such a loss, and they were so sorry. I kept repeating "Thank you for coming" like one of those dolls that squeaks out a few words when you pull the string in its back.

Whenever someone new arrived, Grandma burst into a fresh flood of tears. How could she cry so much for Dad when she hardly ever saw him when he was alive, while I, who'd lost the two most important people in my life, couldn't scare up a single tear? When Mrs. Winkler served coffee and the cake the teachers brought, I slipped away to my room and plopped down in the puddle of late-afternoon sunshine spilling through the window onto my bed.

The bed seemed to pull me down into it. I'd hardly slept since the crash because I was afraid to close my eyes at night. Like staying on guard in the dark would keep horrible things from happening. Although what could possibly be more horrible than what had already happened?

Now the sun was so bright that I dared to doze off. When I woke again, the sympathy callers were gone. My door was partly open. I could hear Grandma and Aunt Alice talking in the living room. Grandma said, "Lisa is my only grandchild.

She is all the family I have left. You can't refuse me the comfort of having her with me at the memorial service." Her voice was thick with tears.

Aunt Alice made that sound in her throat that I was learning meant I'm-trying-to-be-patient-but-not-making-a-very-good-job-of-it. She said, "I'm not refusing. I'm simply pointing out that Lisa's needs may be different from yours. Mine certainly are."

Grandma blew her nose. I was coming to know that sound well, too. She argued, "The airline offered to fly us to England free of charge."

"I don't want their blood money."

Grandma insisted that the airline was just trying to help. She described how appropriate, how dignified, how beautiful the memorial service would be. Her droning voice was punctuated by Aunt Alice's impatient throat sounds.

Aunt Alice finally broke in, "I'm sure going to London will be a comfort to you. Personally, I'd rather have my teeth drilled without Novocain. But we're talking about Lisa. We should let her decide."

"She is too young to decide such an important thing."

Aunt Alice cleared her throat again. "Lisa is not too young to have strong feelings about it."

Aunt Alice was wrong. I didn't have strong feelings about going to the memorial. I didn't have any feelings at all. I felt like I'd been turned into a solid block of marble. You could carve me into a statue.

I lost what little interest I'd had in the argument. My eyes closed and I drifted off again. I slept and dreamed that I was watching a young woman in a long white dress walking through a garden of bright flowers and leafy herbs. The air was filled with their fragrance. Although I'm a city girl who can barely tell a daisy from a geranium, in my dream I knew the names of all the plants: thyme, oxlip, violets, woodbine, musk roses, and eglantine. The young woman strolled toward a picture-postcard thatched cottage. As the hem of her long dress brushed the flowers, they flew up like butterflies to settle on her long auburn hair, making a crown for her. I had the feeling that I knew her from somewhere, that I knew her well, but I couldn't remember who she was. She beckoned to me to follow her.

chapter
3

Our plane to London was supposed to leave at eight at night, but takeoffs were delayed by a thunderstorm. Aunt Alice paced the waiting area like a lion in a cage. Grandma fussed with her carry-on bags and worried about missing the memorial service. I sat and stared into space. I'd only agreed to go to the service to stop Grandma's crying. It was all the same to me if I sat in my room, at the airport, in a London hotel, or on a rock in the Painted Desert.

Aunt Alice wandered off and came back declaring angrily, "Security in this airport is ridiculous. An old man set the metal detector alarm off. When he was on the other side, he pulled a key ring out of his pocket. The guard waved him on without his going through the machine again. He could have been carrying anything! My sister's plane is blown up by a terrorist bomb and this is what the airlines call security."

She went on and on about it. Why was she getting herself in such a stew? What difference did airport security make now? Anyway, I was too exhausted to listen.

Grandma had warned me to get a good night's sleep before the trip because it would be hard to sleep on the plane. Good advice if weird thoughts aren't waiting to pounce on you in the dark. I did try. I lay in bed with my eyes closed for half an hour. Then I snapped the lamp on and read *A Midsummer Night's Dream* as if I could still please Mom by doing my homework. I read all night, until it started to get light and I could safely put the book down.

When our plane finally took off, I discovered that Grandma was right: it's impossible to sleep on a plane even if you aren't afraid of awful things happening if you don't keep watch. You can't lie down and there is no room for your feet. So I watched the movie. That is, I think I watched the movie. I can't remember what it was called or what it was about. I do remember walking out of the terminal at Heathrow Airport into a bright morning while my watch still said the middle of the night and being surprised that the world was still there. But I didn't feel part of it.

I was so spacey the whole time we were in London that the days there are a blur. My memory loss isn't all bad. It's a shame to barely remember walking across a bridge (was it London Bridge?) to get a better view of Big Ben. It's not such a shame to forget Grandma and the other relatives clinging to one another and sobbing at the memorial service.

I remember Aunt Alice telling Grandma that she'd go crazy if she didn't get away from all the grief for a while. She said she was going on a bus tour to Stratford-upon-Avon and taking me with her. I half remember a long bus ride through the countryside. Then I was in a crowd of tourists in a whitewashed, low-ceilinged room in a house the guide said was Shakespeare's birthplace. The guide described the furniture. The tourists pushed and shoved to see better. They were breathing up all the air, not leaving any for me.

I asked Aunt Alice, "Can we go outside? I'm a little dizzy."

Aunt Alice is a good pusher. She cleared a path for us and sat me down on a bench in the Shakespeare garden. After I'd sat a while, she said, "Some exercise will probably make you feel better. Let's walk across the fields to Anne Hathaway's cottage."

"You go. I'll rest here."

She said she'd stay with me. I insisted she go. She didn't take much persuading. She hurried off, promising she wouldn't be long.

I sat quietly on the bench with my hands folded in my

lap. It was a misty day. The air was like a transparent curtain softening the edges of the world. Every now and then the sun broke through to highlight the colors of the flowers. There seemed to be more flowers in the garden than when I sat down. I hadn't noticed that one before. It looked like a small purple velvet face. Its name was on the tip of my tongue.

"That is love-in-idleness."

I turned toward the voice. A girl of my own age in a long white dress was sitting on the bench next to me. Although she looked familiar, I couldn't place her. But the flower's name popped into my head. "Back home, we call it a pansy."

She told me, "If you want a man to love you, you rub its juice on his eyelids whilst he sleeps. Only you must be careful that you are the first thing he sees when he wakes."

I added, "Or he'll fall in love with an ass's head. I know *A Midsummer Night's Dream*, too."

"Do you?" She seemed delighted. "I am the person who told Will how to use the herb to charm love. Then he put it in his play. He says 'tis pity I am a girl because I have such fine ideas."

I said, "Sure. You know William Shakespeare personally."

"I beg pardon. I should have introduced myself. I am his cousin, Rowena Shakespeare. My friends call me Rooji."

Rooji? So that's why she looked so familiar. But how . . . ? I was totally confused. I shook my head to clear it.

She answered my head shake, "We are sitting in the garden of Cousin Will's house."

I turned to look at the house behind me. Sure enough, it was Shakespeare's birthplace. Although the white stucco looked freshly painted, it was the same house I had fled to escape the crush of tourists a few minutes ago. Only now there were no tour buses, no tourists, no guides herding them in and out. "Cousin Will?" I repeated stupidly. "Your Cousin Will is William Shakespeare?"

"Did you see him act in *Love's Labour Lost* at the inn last autumn? I pleaded with Uncle until he let me attend, although he says that a play is no place for a young maid. Forsooth, it was wonderful! I forgot I was watching Cousin Will's company of actors. I thought that I was truly among the lords and ladies in the court of Navarre and I was taking part in the merriment of the wooing. When the last notes of the owl's song died away, I cried because I had to return to ordinary life."

It was impossible for her to have seen Shakespeare act. He lived four hundred years ago. But it was also impossible for his birthplace to suddenly look new and for the tourists to have disappeared. Also, Rooji would never lie to me.

She was waiting for me to say something. The best I could do was, "I've never seen a Shakespeare play, but I'm reading one for school."

"I can read. Cousin Will taught me; I was ever his pet. Before he went back to London, he gave me a book of tales told by pilgrims on the road to Canterbury. Aunt told him that girls have no need for reading, that it puts ideas into their heads and makes them discontented with their proper place in life. Mayhaps she was right. Ever since I attended the play, while my hands churned butter or stirred the stew, my heart dreamed of running away to become an actor as Will did. Now that spring has come, the plague has gone, and the London theaters are open again, all I can think about is that some company must need a 'prentice actor."

"I hate to tell you this, but in Shakespeare's day girls couldn't go on the stage. The women's parts were played by boy actors." I knew that from my English report.

She looked like I'd made a point of telling her that grass was green. "That is why I must dress in boys' clothes when I go to London." She laughed. "Would it not be a good jest if I joined Cousin Will's company and fooled him with my disguise?"

Was she playing a "good jest" on me? To find out, I questioned her carefully about "Cousin Will's company." If it turned out that she was putting me on, I'd say I was just going along with the joke.

Her answers all checked out with what I'd read for my report. She even knew how many actors owned shares in Shakespeare's company and where he got the ideas for his plays. Strange as it seemed, I found myself believing that she really was William Shakespeare's cousin.

Suddenly she stood up. "Talking to you has made up my mind. I will leave this very hour to seek my fortune in the theater. Today is market day. I can fetch some of Will's old clothes while Aunt is still at market. I will change clothes in the woods and be on my way to London before I am missed." She gathered up her full skirts and asked, "Mayhaps you will come with me?"

A few weeks ago, the girls I ate lunch with cut afternoon classes to watch Tom Cruise film a movie on Fifth Avenue. Although I was dying to go with them, I couldn't bring myself to break the rules. So I muttered something about a test. They didn't bother trying to persuade me because I was already down in their books as a wimp.

Here was my chance to prove I wasn't a wimp. "I'll go if you really want me. And if you can get me some clothes, too. I can't run around Elizabethan England in jeans and a sweatshirt."

Rummaging through Rooji's aunt's clothes chest was like getting ready for a costume party. (At least, what I imagine it's like. Nobody ever invited me to one.) Will's old clothes were strange enough to be costumes. What looked like striped girls' tights turned out to be boys' *hose*. Rooji helped me find *points* (sort of like shoe laces) to attach my hose to my *doublet* (fitted jacket).

As we rolled our disguises into bundles, I wished the girls at school could see me. They had only cut afternoon classes. I was in a strange country, in a strange century, running away to a glorious adventure. I was dizzy with freedom.

Rooji picked up her bundle and opened the door to the garden. I asked, "Aren't you going to leave your parents a note so they'll know you weren't kidnapped or something?"

"My mother and father died in the plague last year. I live with Aunt and Uncle now."

"I'm so sorry! I didn't know." I felt terrible about reminding her. I felt terrible for her. I felt so terrible that I started to cry. It was the strangest thing: I hadn't cried for my own parents, but I wept for Rooji's loss.

She said, "It is God's will."

I sobbed, "Why should He want to take your mom and dad?"

She answered, "I don't know," and burst into tears, too.

We cried together, hugging each other for comfort the way we used to when I was little.

Rooji wiped her eyes with the back of her hand. I dug a tissue out of my jeans' pocket and gave it to her. She looked puzzled. I said, "Like this," and blew my nose in another tissue. She blew right through hers and looked so surprised that I couldn't help giggling.

She grabbed my hand and pulled me out the door. We ran through the garden and out into the fields. In a few minutes, we reached the forest and made our way to a clearing. Rooji dropped to the grass gasping, "Corsets may shape us for beauty, but they make running difficult."

While she caught her breath, I explored the clearing. I hadn't been in a forest since I was a kid in summer camp. When the counselor took us on forest hikes, I'd always imagined wonderful things waiting in the trees for me to step off the path and find them.

Rooji called, "Don't walk there. That faint circle in the grass is a fairy ring. The fairies' footsteps made it when they danced here at midnight."

I smiled at anyone believing such stuff. However, I was careful where I stepped.

Rooji untied the laces of her dress. "Let us hasten to

change and be on our way. Else darkness will catch us still in the forest."

Her dress came apart like a skirt and blouse—only the sleeves were separate, too. Underneath she wore a wire thing to hold her skirt out, two petticoats, and a corset over what looked like a cotton nightgown. No wonder she wanted to dress like a boy. Although boys' clothes were pretty complicated, too, as I found out when I put mine on.

Rooji hid our regular clothes under a bush. With her long hair tucked into a feathered cap, it was amazing how much like a boy she looked. But she'd always been able to change her shape and sex when she wanted.

As I followed her along a path that snaked through the tall trees, I asked, "How far is it to London?"

"Nigh eighty miles as the crow flies."

"We can't walk eighty miles!"

"Mayhaps we will not have to walk the whole way. Once we reach the road on the other side of the forest, some farmer may give two likely lads a ride in his cart. Walking or riding, with a little luck we should reach London in less than a week."

A week! For a trip Aunt Alice and I did in less than a morning by bus. Why, we'd flown from New York to London in only seven hours.

Surprisingly, I found myself enjoying our slow pace. In a plane, even if you have a window seat, you mostly see clouds. In a bus on the highway, you watch the houses and trees zip past at fifty-five miles an hour. On foot, you are close to everything. I stopped to smell the wild roses just coming into bloom. I picked tiny, sweet wild strawberries and washed them down with cool water from a sparkling stream. The peace of the forest soothed me.

After a while, Rooji said, "Let us tell stories to amuse ourselves as we walk. I know a story about a cowardly king and a princess who was as brave as a lion."

Not a very promising plot, but I soon saw why she was

desperate to go on the stage. She was a wonderful actress. When she played the king cowering under his throne in terror, you wanted to drag him out. When she was the princess wearing the king's armor to lead his army into battle, you wanted to leap up and follow her. When she finished the princess's final speech praising the soldiers for defending their country's honor, I clapped until my palms stung.

Rooji took a deep bow, sweeping off her cap and holding it over her heart. Her long hair tumbled down in a coppery wave. I always wanted hair that color. Mine is a boring brown.

She brushed the bright strands away from her face. "My hair will fall down and betray me. You must cut it."

I protested, "Oh, no. It's so beautiful."

"I would cut off my ears to be an actor." She sat down on a tree stump and handed me a pair of scissors. (Where had she gotten them?) "Tell me a story while you cut."

After her performance, I'd sound as interesting as a math lesson. But I had to distract her from the scissors snipping off the bright locks of her hair. "Once there was a girl named Dorothy who had a dog named Toto . . ." I've seen *The Wizard of Oz* on TV every year since I was four. I summarized the story and sang the songs.

Rooji said she'd never heard such delightful music. She made me sing "Somewhere Over the Rainbow" again. Then she said, "That was beautiful. We will join the same acting company. You can sing while I act."

Although I sing in the school chorus, that's a long way from being good enough for the theater. But it was fun to pretend it might happen. After all, stranger things had already happened.

When Rooji's hair was trimmed to a neat pageboy, we set off down a narrow path that ran through thick walls of green trees. We walked on and on. I was getting tired and our steady pace through the quiet forest lulled me into a kind of trance. I didn't notice that the light was fading until Rooji plucked at my jacket and whispered, "Night is falling."

Automatically, I glanced at my watch, forgetting that I'd hidden it under a bush with my jeans and sweatshirt. Then I thought: Without a watch, there is no time. It was a lovely idea.

Rooji asked anxiously, "What shall we do?"

Spotting a mossy bank that appeared next to the path, I answered, "That moss looks soft. We can sleep here tonight and start out again in the morning." I plopped down. I'd called it right; it was soft. My eyelids grew heavy.

Rooji shook my shoulder. "Do not sleep. Fairies roam the forest at night to cast spells and play tricks on unwary travelers."

Already half asleep, I murmured, "We're perfectly safe here. This is a special place. Nothing bad can happen to me here."

She kept shaking me. She was so persistent that I reluctantly opened my eyes.

I was back in the Shakespeare garden. Aunt Alice was saying, "You must have been totally exhausted to fall asleep on a wooden bench. I hate to wake you, but our bus is leaving for London in a few minutes."

chapter
4

I slept on the bus to London and on the plane back to New York. When we got home, I crawled into bed at six at night and slept through until ten the next morning. When I finally got up, Grandma was packing to go back to Phoenix. So soon? With everything that had happened, it was hard to keep track of the days. Time was all mixed up in my head.

I offered to help Grandma pack. It was slow going because she kept deciding that something we'd just put in her suitcase should go in her carry-on bag, or the other way around. We still were not finished when Aunt Alice came in to announce that Grandma's taxi was on its way. Aunt Alice stuffed the rest of the things in any which way and closed up the bags.

Grandma hugged me tight against her pillowy chest and sobbed, "You poor baby. I can't bear leaving you." She was suffocating me, but I didn't pull away. I had little enough to cling to.

Aunt Alice detached Grandma and handed her a tissue. Grandma blew her nose loudly. It reminded me of Rooji's trouble with tissues. Then I was filled with confusion. What was I thinking of? It was crazy to believe I'd run away with Shakespeare's cousin. But it was hard to convince myself that I'd only dreamed it. My adventure with Rooji was more real to me than Mom and Dad being dead.

Dead. That was the first time I'd even thought the awful word. Shuddering, I made myself concentrate on what Grandma was saying.

"Lisa, darling, I wish with all my heart that you could come live with me, but only seniors are allowed in my retirement community. Although grandchildren can visit, they mustn't stay longer than a month."

Living in Phoenix with Grandma had never occurred to me. This was my home. I assured her, "I understand. We'll talk on the phone. And I'll come visit you real soon."

Grandma sniffed back fresh tears. "You are such a sweet child. It breaks my heart to go."

Aunt Alice made her impatient throat sound.

Grandma turned to her. "I worry about leaving Lisa with you. It's such a responsibility to bring up a child. You are hardly more than a child yourself."

"I'm thirty-one."

"That may seem a great age to you. When you are as old as I am . . ."

Grandma's taxi honked. Aunt Alice carried out Grandma's suitcase, carry-on bag, garment bag, and the shopping bag full of Dad's diplomas and stuff. She settled Grandma and her luggage into the cab. We stood on the curb and waved as it pulled away. Aunt Alice was clearly glad to be rid of Grandma's fussing and crying. But Grandma was half the family I had left. I felt lonely and abandoned.

We went back upstairs. Aunt Alice made herself a cup of Red Zinger tea with honey. (She thinks caffeine and sugar are poison.) I took a glass of milk and a piece of the leftover cake. We sat down at the kitchen table. The table was sticky. She'd never wiped it after breakfast. Without Grandma, the apartment was very quiet and empty.

I watched Aunt Alice brush the crumbs from her breakfast toast into little piles as she sipped her tea. She pushed the piles together and then broke them up again. Watching her was kind of hypnotic. My mind wandered. I began to feel sleepy again. Maybe if I slept, I'd dream . . .

Aunt Alice brought me fully awake. "Are you ready to go?"

I stammered, "Go where?"

"To my house. Just pack a few days' clothes. We'll come back for the rest of your things later."

Her house? I just stared at her.

"Lisa, we discussed this in London. I told you that your parents wanted you to live with me if anything ever happened to them. And you agreed. Remember?"

I didn't remember. I hardly remembered anything about London. But I knew I'd never agreed. Or if I had, it was because I'd been too spacey to know what I was doing. My voice shook as I said, "I've lived in this apartment all my life. It's my home."

"I'm sorry. I understand how you feel. But I must get back to my office. Dr. Sung has covered for me for more than a week. I can't ask her to do it any longer."

It's easy to say you're sorry whether you are or not. She couldn't possibly understand how I felt. I begged, "Can't we stay here a few more days?"

"I really must go back. Dr. Sung has only dealt with emergencies. She postponed my routine appointments. They are all waiting for me."

"I see." I didn't see. I didn't see how this could be happening. I stood up and walked toward my room like a windup toy. Halfway through the doorway, the toy ran down. I turned and tried, "Aunt Alice . . ." But I couldn't think of anything more to say. There was nothing to say or do.

She asked, "How would you feel about skipping the 'aunt' and just calling me Alice?"

My mother and father were . . . gone. My grandmother was in Phoenix. And Alice wouldn't even let me keep an aunt. Not that she'd win any prizes for being an aunt. I answered stiffly, "My mother didn't approve of my being familiar with my elders."

The throat-clearing sound. Then she said, "Why don't you think about what *you* would like to call me?"

I didn't answer. I ran into my room and jammed underwear, socks, and shirts into my backpack. From now on, I wouldn't call her anything. Not even "Hey you."

When the backpack was full, I dumped it out again and folded my shirts neatly so they wouldn't get creased. *Her* clothes always looked like she didn't own an iron. I didn't want people to think I was a slob like her.

◆━◆━◆

To make leaving my home even harder, she lived in Brooklyn. For Manhattan people like me, Brooklyn might as well be Peoria. The cabdriver's scowl as she gave the address made it clear that he thought so, too.

On the way, she gave me a real estate agent spiel about her neighborhood. She said she lived right near Prospect Park, which was great for jogging, biking, or just walking. She described the nearby library and botanical gardens, the trendy shops and restaurants, and the convenient subway that would take me to my school in Manhattan in a half hour. I didn't answer. I just stared out the cab window, hugging my misery to myself. When the cab swerved while passing another car on the Brooklyn Bridge, I hoped we'd crash through the guardrail and plunge into the river below.

We pulled up in front of a three-story brownstone. As we climbed the high stoop to the front door, she told me that this row of houses was a hundred years old, a landmark. She said that her apartment was on the old parlor floor and her office was in the semibasement that used to be the kitchen and servants' hall. After the history lesson, the inside was a surprise. White walls, modern furniture, and track lighting. One light shone on a large painting made up of bright, swirling colors.

She saw me looking at the picture. "That was a farewell present from an artist I used to live with. Someday it might be worth more than the share of the rent he never paid."

Embarrassed by her talking to me like I was her girlfriend, I asked, "Where do I sleep?"

She led me into a cramped little room that looked like it hadn't been vacuumed since the Vietnam War. There were dust balls in the corners and junk scattered all over the place. An angora cat was washing its paws on the Hide-A-Bed. At least the cat was making an effort to be clean.

She said, "It's a bit of a mess now, but we'll fix it up for you. A paint job, curtains, posters. Do kids still like posters?"

"I don't."

She persisted. "What color paint would you like?"

"What I'd like is to go home." I don't know how I managed to sound like my mother talking to a saleswoman who was showing her inferior merchandise. I guess I was desperate. The room was awful. I couldn't live in it.

She looked at me thoughtfully. I could practically hear the wheels spinning in her head. Then she said, "I think we should talk. Sit down."

The heroine of a book would have said, "I'd rather stand." I sat down on the Hide-A-Bed. The cat jumped into my lap. I ran my hand over its silky fur. I could never have a cat or dog at home because animal hair gave my father an asthma attack.

She turned the desk chair around and straddled it. Why couldn't she sit like a normal person? She said, "Bathsheba likes you. You should be flattered. She is very choosy about her friends."

I kept my eyes on the cat as I stroked it. I had to sit and listen. I didn't have to make it easy for her.

"Lisa, I know how terrible everything has been for you. It's like a nightmare you can't wake up from."

She didn't know. She couldn't know. Nobody could know. I cuddled the cat in silence.

She said, "You have to understand that this is hard for me, too. I want to do the right thing. I want to help you. But I can't keep trying to guess what you need. You have to tell me."

I didn't answer. She was the grown-up. She was supposed to know what to do. My mother and father always knew. I needed them back. I needed things the way they were before. I clung to the cat, squeezing it so hard that it yowled. I let it loose. It jumped down and scampered away. Cats aren't loyal like dogs. Dogs never abandon you no matter what you do.

"Lisa, talk to me!"

"What do you want me to say?"

Her face got a tight, pulled-down look, like she had a sudden stomachache. I knew she was angry, but she controlled herself and said, "Okay. We'll leave it for now." She gathered up scattered copies of *Veterinary Medicine.* "Here. Put these in the living room bookcase."

There was no room in the bookcase. I had to stuff the magazines in across the tops of the books. Then I sat down in a big leather armchair. I didn't want to go back into that awful room. And I didn't want to talk to her. She couldn't make me.

Or could she? My parents had appointed her my guardian, which meant she was supposed to take care of me. What if she got really mad and decided she didn't want the responsibility? Mom and Dad had given me to her, but did she have to keep me? As miserable as I was about living with her, it was even worse to imagine her sending me away. Where would I go?

To shut off those frightening thoughts, I tried to figure out the painting the guy she'd lived with had left instead of the rent. It didn't seem to be a picture of anything. Just swirling colors. But once I started staring at it, I couldn't tear my eyes away. I had to follow the brown swirl to where it disappeared into the green, and the green swirl to where it became blue. It was hypnotic, like a whirlpool sucking me in.

Rooji's voice said, "Look. We are coming into London."

chapter 5

The open cart hit a deep rut in the road, throwing me off the sack of turnips that served as my seat. I fell onto a covered basket that squawked indignantly. The farmer who had given us a lift turned to scold, "Mind the goose." Like I was lying on it on purpose. As I struggled back into my seat, we hit another rut. I landed on my butt on the bottom of the cart. Rooji was sitting comfortably on her sack in spite of our being bounced around like corn in a popper. She giggled.

I laughed, too. A pratfall is funny, even if you are the one taking it. Only after I was back on my sack did I wonder how I'd gotten here. Not only how I got from Aunt Alice's living room to Rooji's England, but how I got into this bone-jolting cart. I'd left Rooji in the forest near Stratford. Now we were coming into London. Could I have forgotten a weeklong journey?

Rooji seemed to accept my being here with her now without question. She bounced up and down on her sack in excitement. "I cannot believe that I am finally in London."

Her excitement was catching. I said, "It'll be fun to see all the things I missed last time."

"Have you been to London before? When?"

"I was here with my aunt and grandmother . . ." I almost added, "last week," but that wasn't right. If now was really four hundred years ago, then I'd left London a few days less than four hundred years from now. But that didn't sound right either.

There was no sense worrying about it. I'd always worried about every little thing, and what had it gotten me? I said, "Let's go see the crown jewels and the changing of the guard at Buckingham Palace."

Rooji nodded happily. "What number of wonders there must be in London town. Cousin Will never mentioned the ones you speak of."

As our cart rattled through the streets, I saw why Cousin Will and I had different lists of London sights. Shakespeare's London was like a sprawling village of two- and three-story houses with some churches thrown in. The streets were narrow and crowded.

Living in Manhattan, I'm used to busy streets. But at home people are all hurrying someplace. Here they were doing things right in the street: plucking chickens, mending pots, making jewelry, and waving their wares under the noses of the passersby. People dodged around the stalls, the pushcarts, one another. It was like a show put on especially for me.

The farmer asked what part of London we were headed for. When Rooji said "The Bankside," he warned, "That be no place for country lads. It be full of rogues and vagabonds and lazy 'prentices shirking work to see plays and bear baiting."

Rooji told him we were going to her cousin who was an actor.

The farmer shrugged to show his low opinion of actors. Then he stopped the cart and pointed. "Go that way, acrost London Bridge."

He had pointed straight. The narrow streets didn't run straight. They twisted and turned and ran into even narrower alleys or dead ends. In no time we were completely lost.

Rooji fretted about finding the theaters, but I was enjoying myself too much to care. There was so much to see and do. Shopkeepers shouted to us that their ribbons or trinkets were the prettiest, their bread or sweetmeats the tastiest. They begged us to stop for a drink, a haircut, a tooth pulled. I watched a blacksmith making a horseshoe, his hammer striking sparks from the red-hot metal. Then we joined the crowd around an open-air puppet show where Judy beat Punch over the head with a stick while grubby children shouted at her to hit harder.

London was a great place to wander through—if you were careful where you stepped (ugh!) and you didn't mind being shoved. People pushed past without a warning or apology. Three boys, in particular, seemed to make a science of being rude. They came down the narrow street singing at the top of their lungs. I recognized the type. At home they wear metallic T-shirts and blast their boom boxes on the crowded bus. Here they wore doublets and linked arms to force everyone out of their way. Rooji and I backed against the wall of a house to let them pass.

I don't know what got into me. I'm usually careful to avoid trouble. I stuck out my foot without stopping to think that being dressed as a boy I might get punched out. The nearest one tripped over my foot, righted himself, and scowled at me. Then he laughed and continued on his noisy way. Although his teeth were crooked (braces hadn't been invented yet), he had a nice smile.

Rooji said, "I see a *cook-shop* down that street. Are you hungry?"

A cook-shop turned out to be a sixteenth-century fast-food place. It sold hot meat *pasties* (small pies). Like the Burger King near school, it was jammed. Only there were no lines. It was grab what you can.

Rooji waited to buy our pasties. And waited. She missed chance after chance to push up to the counter. She had clearly never ridden the Lexington Avenue subway at rush hour. Unless I wanted to starve, it was up to me. I took two pennies (pennies!) from her and waded in.

I followed in the wake of a tall boy in a blue doublet (a

trick I'd learned on the subway). As he reached the cook handing out the pasties, I darted in front of him—and recognized the boy I'd tripped before. He recognized me, too, and threatened, "Plague me again, brat, and I crack your head." But he let me take his place when he'd gotten his food.

Why do things that are supposed to be bad for you taste so good? I never ate anything as delicious as the hot, crisp, fried pasties that Rooji and I gobbled outside the cook-shop.

The boy in blue and his friends were eating theirs a short distance away. The blue boy looked like he knew his way around. I licked the grease and crumbs off my fingers and went up to him. "Can you tell me how to get to the Bankside?"

"What do babes like you want with the Bankside?"

"We're looking for the playhouses."

"Know you not that plays are bad influences? They lure 'prentices from work and fill their heads with improper ideas." He grinned and his friends guffawed loudly.

I looked down my nose at him. (Which was hard to do because he was a head taller.) "My friend's cousin is a famous actor."

"And Richard Burbage is my uncle."

I was tempted to tell him that I didn't know who Richard Whosis was, but Rooji's cousin was more than an actor. He was the greatest playwright in the world. Instead I said stiffly, "If you'll just direct us to London Bridge, we'll find our way from there."

He turned to his friends. "What say we corrupt these babes?" Without waiting for an answer (he was the leader) he ordered, "Come along with us. Mind you walk smartly. Else we be late for the play."

He said his name was Ned. The other boys were Tom and Henry. Rooji introduced us as Robin and Lee. Ned was learning to be a silversmith in his father's shop. His friends were apprenticed to a tailor. They had sneaked off from work this afternoon to see a play called *The Revenge of Pavia*. They'd heard it had lots of swordplay.

Ned and his friends linked arms with us. Now there were five of us forming a human roadblock. We ran shouting and laughing through the maze of streets. Most people stood aside to let us pass, but one angry man swung a stick at us and another threatened us with his sword. The boys acted like it was all great fun. Surprisingly, it was.

Finally Ned pointed. "There it be. London Bridge."

The bridge looked like a city street continuing across the river. Two rows of shops ran all the way across with a church in the middle. I noticed Rooji gazing up openmouthed. My eyes followed hers to the top of the first arch. My mind refused to believe what my eyes saw. Those had to be furry bowling balls on hockey sticks. I stammered, "Are they . . .?"

Ned finished my sentence, "The heads of criminals stuck on pikes." He added with relish, "They stay there until they rot. First the birds peck out their eyes. Then . . . Why, babe, your face is turning green."

I declared, "Those awful things would turn any normal person's stomach. It's disgusting."

Ned shrugged. "It is a warning to all wrongdoers." Tom and Henry nodded. Even Rooji agreed that such things were necessary.

Couldn't they see how horrible it was? Then I thought: Is it more horrible than *Newsweek* printing full-color pictures of bodies being dragged out of a wrecked plane? Maybe things are only horrible when you're not used to them. Maybe you can get used to anything.

Ned said, "Enough gawking if we want good places for the play."

The Theatre (that was its name, The Theatre) was a long walk from the other side of London Bridge. I never dreamed how far people walked before cars and subways. My legs were a solid ache by the time we reached the round building with the flag flying from its roof. The others sprinted the last yards as if we hadn't tramped for miles. Only the thought of finally plopping into a seat helped me to keep up with them.

There were no seats. At least not where we were. In a Broadway theater we'd be in the orchestra, the most expensive seats in the house. Here it was the cheapest section (admission: one penny) and you were lucky to have room to stand on the rushes that covered the wooden floor.

Ned used the pushing skill he'd shown in the cook-shop to stake out places for us near the stage. He and Tom and Henry held our ground against challenges from other hookey-playing 'prentices. I looked around curiously, imagining my teacher's reaction if I told her I'd actually been in a theater like the one I wrote about in my English report.

The stage, which had no curtain, jutted out into the audience like an off-Broadway theater-in-the-round. But this theater had no roof in the middle. I could see why the three tiers of balconies were more expensive than the pit where we were. Not only did the balconies have stools for people to sit on, they were covered in case it started to rain.

The boys and men around me (there were no girls or women in the pit) ate and drank and called to the orange sellers and to one another like schoolkids carrying on in the cafeteria when the teacher on duty is called away. Since there were no houselights to dim or curtain to go up, there was no hush before the play began. The audience's noise only died down a little when a trumpet blew three times to announce the start of the action. Some actors in soldiers' helmets came onstage discussing a war between two countries whose names I didn't catch.

With all the racket around me, I couldn't follow the complicated plot. I whispered to Rooji, "I wish people would shut up. You're supposed to be quiet in a theater."

She asked "Why?" like she had never heard of such a thing.

"Because they're making so much noise I can't follow what's happening."

Rooji filled me in. It seemed that the prince of Pavia had been kidnapped as a baby by the king of Malfi. That meant that the enemy the prince was fighting was his real country and that the other prince, the one he met in the hermit's cave, was really his brother.

The two princes made angry speeches. They exchanged insults, calling each other things like "puckfist" and "blatherskite." That sounded funny to me, but the audience took it all very seriously. They called out some insults they thought the princes might not know. When the princes drew their swords to duel, the audience burst into shouts of "Kill him" and "Run him through."

Ned backed the kidnapped prince. "Attack. Aim for the heart."

Tom and Henry rooted for the other one, shouting, "Stand your ground. Parry and cut over."

Rooji couldn't make up her mind, so she egged them both on.

I got tired of being the only person in the place behaving properly. When in London, do as the Londoners do. I yelled, "Stop fighting. You're really brothers." It was fun being involved.

The boys howled for a duel to the death, but I was glad nobody got killed. The kidnapped prince won, everything got straightened out, and the play ended in a victory celebration with songs and dances.

Rooji didn't think much of the ladies (really boy actors) who were singing. She announced, "Lisa . . . I mean Lee, sings better than they do." She urged me to sing along so our new friends could hear how good I was. I said I didn't know the words. She told me to do the "Hey nonny nonny" part. I said my throat was sore from yelling.

In back of us, one of the 'prentices who had tried to grab our places said loudly, "He makes excuses because, forsooth, he caws like an ugsome crow."

Ned told him in fancy sixteenth-century language to shut up because I sang like a nightingale. The other boy answered with a raspy "Caw caw." Ned said he'd rather be a crow than a "puerile poxied pig." I thought it was going to end with a Shakespearean version of "How would you like a knuckle sandwich?" Instead they settled for "Put your money where your mouth is."

The bet was on. Ned, Tom, and Henry backed my voice with their hard-earned pennies. The other 'prentices covered the bet and shouted for higher stakes. Rooji dug into her doublet for four more pennies, all the money she had left. An older boy who sang in a church choir was appointed as judge. Then they all waited for me to sing.

The chorus teacher at school once asked me to do a solo, but I was scared to sing alone with everyone staring at me. And nobody's last pennies were riding on my performance then. Now my mouth went dry as sand and my legs threatened to buckle under me.

Ned encouraged me, "Sing out, Lee."

I couldn't croak out a note.

Rooji urged, "Sing the rainbow song."

Scared as I was, I couldn't let Rooji and Ned and Tom and Henry lose all their money. I couldn't let them down. I licked my dry lips and forced myself to take three deep breaths. Then I gave it everything I had. "Somewhere over the rainbow, bluebirds fly . . ."

I did it! Rooji was hugging me. Ned was pounding me on the back. Henry was collecting our winnings, and Tom was shouting to the orange seller for five of her biggest oranges.

I felt wonderful. I wanted to stand there with my friends making a fuss over me forever. But my aching legs refused to hold me up any longer. I murmured, "My kingdom for a chair," and sank down onto the rushes.

chapter
6

lice said, "So you're a floor-sitter, too. At least we have something in common."

Startled, I looked up. What was Alice doing in the theater? Then I saw the picture over the sofa. I wasn't in the theater anymore. I was sitting on the rug in Alice's living room, and my friends were gone.

I told myself that I must have dozed off and had another vivid dream. I didn't want to believe it. I wanted to be back with Rooji in the wonderful world of yesterday. Maybe if I threw my eyes out of focus the way you do with those Magic Eye 3-D pictures, I'd look right through Alice into Rooji's world.

Alice stayed stubbornly solid. She said, "I'm surprised your mother didn't teach you to sit on a chair like a lady. She was always after me." She dropped to the rug in a single smooth motion, ending cross-legged in the yoga lotus position.

I had always wanted to learn yoga. For a second, I was tempted to ask her to show me how she did that. But I couldn't let her remark about my mother go past. Saying, "Mom did teach me," I scrambled awkwardly to my feet. Then I sat down properly in the big armchair. Or as properly as it permitted. It was the kind of chair that makes you lean back whether or not you want to.

Alice frowned but didn't say anything. We sat in silence for a minute. She comfortably cross-legged on the rug, I stiffly in the chair. Then she told me, "I left sheets, a blanket, and a pillow on the Hide-A-Bed. You can make it up when you're ready."

I'd never be ready. I said, "Okay."

More silence. I had time to puzzle over my adventure with Rooji. I'd heard of recurrent dreams—having the same dream over and over. I'd never heard of a dream that picked up where the last one left off. Also, dreams were usually all mixed-up. I'd never had a dream that made perfect sense and that I remembered perfectly. Maybe it had really happened. There were lots of books about people going into different worlds. There was *Alice in Wonderland* and *Back to the Future* and . . .

Alice interrupted my thoughts. She rose easily to her feet without using her hands. "I have to see to the animals. How about coming down to the office with me?"

"No, thank you."

She cleared her throat. I was getting to hate that sound. "I could use some help."

It was just like her to make it sound like an invitation and then act like I was lazy when I refused. I wanted to tell her that Mom used to boast to Mrs. Winkler that I never had to be asked twice to clear the table or fold the laundry. But she'd think I was making excuses.

I followed her down the narrow stairs that led to the office's back entrance. I'd never been in a vet's office before. It would have been interesting to see the examining and operating rooms. She didn't bother to give me a tour. She stopped in a room with cages like a pet shop. Two of the cages were occupied. The Peke in the first one yapped shrilly when it saw us. A floppy-eared beagle lay in the other cage staring through the mesh with mournful eyes.

She examined the Peke, feeling his body with expert fingers. I couldn't help admiring the way she handled him. Although Pekes are usually bad-tempered, he let her do whatever she wanted. He even licked her hand. I asked, "What do you want me to do?"

She nodded toward the beagle. "Play with Rex."

"I thought you said you needed help."

"Rex is depressed. You seem to have a way with animals. Bathsheba took to you. Maybe you can get Rex to respond."

Why didn't she say that in the first place? I felt stupid for misunderstanding, even though it was her fault.

The beagle didn't move when I opened his cage. I whistled softly and called his name. He just lay there. I reached in and patted his head gently. He didn't seem to care what I did. I wanted to help him, but I didn't know how. I said, "I never heard of a dog getting depressed."

"Dogs have feelings just like people—only more straightforward. Unlike people, they don't hide their feelings. You never have to guess whether a dog likes you or hates you."

That wasn't fair. I didn't hate her. It was just that she always did the wrong thing. Like making me feel guilty now. I pretended not to understand that she meant me. "Why is Rex unhappy?"

"The couple who raised him from a puppy were transferred overseas and had to leave him behind. Relatives gave Rex a good home, but he couldn't adjust. He stopped eating and refused to have anything to do with them."

"I know how he feels." It just popped out of me.

"Because you feel the same way?"

I started to say, "That's ridiculous." I started to say, "Wouldn't you?" I started to say, "I can't stand you being so different from Mom and Dad. I can't stand everything being so different." I'll never know which I would have said, or if I'd have said anything, because the phone picked that moment to ring.

She said, "Shoot!" and went to answer it. Actually, she used a word I won't repeat. Mom used to say there was no excuse for vulgar language.

I petted Rex with long, firm strokes from his head to his tail. I scratched his floppy ears. I tickled him under his chin. No reaction. It was like playing with a fur coat. He was so thin I could feel his bones under the fur.

The food in his bowl was dried out. I was looking around for something to tempt him with when Alice came back. "That call was from Mr. Gordon, whose son was on the plane with your parents. He is forming a relatives' group. Now that it's been confirmed that a bomb was smuggled onto the plane, he feels that we should pressure the airlines for stronger safety measures. He was as angry as I was when I told him about the old man who waltzed through the metal detector at the airport when we went to London."

I asked, "Do you have a bone or something for Rex?"

She took a box of dog biscuits out of a cabinet and handed me one. I held it near Rex's nose. He sniffed it. I coaxed, "Come on, taste it." He had lost interest.

Alice went on, "Of course, I said I'd help. People like us have a responsibility to see that a tragedy like this never happens again."

What was the point? It had already happened to Mom and Dad. It had happened to me. I waved the biscuit in front of Rex's face. He didn't even blink.

She persisted, "Mr. Gordon will contact the relatives. I said we could have the first meeting of the group here next Sunday." When I still didn't respond, she asked, "Don't you think a relatives' group is a good idea?"

"It's okay."

"How do you really feel?"

"I said it's okay."

"What bothers you about it?"

"Nothing! It's your house and you can invite anyone you want."

Mom would have told me it was not necessary to raise my voice or to be disrespectful. Alice said, "I'm sorry. Just because it makes me feel better to do something, I shouldn't assume you feel the same way. As you said: it's my house, so I'll have the meeting here. But you certainly don't have to take part if you don't want to."

Her apology embarrassed me. Kids say they're sorry to

grown-ups, not the other way around. I said, "I shouldn't have yelled."

"You call that yelling? Obviously you've never heard me sound off when I get angry." She waited for me to smile. When I didn't, she asked, "Would you like to go visit one of your friends on Sunday?"

"No. I'll work on my English report."

chapter
7

W hen the doorbell started ringing on Sunday afternoon, I closed the door to my room and tried to concentrate on the book I was reading. Even cleaned up, the room was awful. Unfortunately, it was the only place I had to get away from Alice's relatives' meeting.

I had gone to the library and taken out a book on everyday life in Elizabethan England, a biography of Shakespeare, and an illustrated guide to theaters in Shakespeare's time. Then I'd holed up with the books. They made a wall between me and Alice. While I was reading, I forgot where I was and what had happened. I felt close to Rooji. I read the books from cover to cover and pored over the pictures.

Alice let me hide in my room with my books. My being out of the way made it easier for her to catch up with her work. When she finally thought to mention my returning to school, I showed her the books and said I needed to finish my English report first. She didn't push it. She didn't even ask to see how far I'd gotten with the report. She just went back to work and left me alone to read.

I read deep into the night. The more bleary-eyed I became, the nearer I felt to Rooji. I began to believe that I could step back into her world if I could only find the opening. I experimented with reading by candlelight—and almost set the bed on fire when I knocked the candle over. But that gave me an idea. I made another trip to the library for a book on hypnotism.

I was trying to follow the directions for hypnotizing

myself when the relatives arrived for the meeting. The book said to relax and concentrate on a shiny object. I stared at my watch until my eyes ached. Nothing happened.

How could I relax with all those people jabbering away in the living room? How could I concentrate with phrases like "terrorist bomb" and "innocent victims" and "give their deaths meaning" slipping through the cracks under my closed door?

The more I tried not to listen, the louder and clearer the voices seemed to become. I stuffed my fingers in my ears. The words still got through, "Give their deaths meaning . . . their deaths . . . their deaths . . ." I ran into the bathroom and turned the sink on full force to blot out the horrible words.

When I finally ventured out of the bathroom, a tall boy was standing near the open door to my room. It was Ned! I was so happy that I nearly threw my arms around him and hugged him. He gestured toward the living room. "I see you're hiding from the circus in there."

Of course he wasn't Ned. How could I have imagined he was? Aside from being tall and having dark curly hair, there was no resemblance. Ned was smiling and full of mischief. This boy looked like he had a grudge against the world.

I muttered, "I'm not hiding." It was none of his business if I was.

"Then why aren't you inside thinking up bright ideas to make the skies safe for Aladdin's carpet and visitors from outer space?"

"My aunt said I didn't have to go to the meeting if I didn't want to. Why did *you* come if you think it's so stupid?"

"My father made me. He organized this whole thing. Like he expects sending petitions to Congress or picketing the airline will bring him back."

"Bring who back?"

He glared at me as if I was supposed to know and was acting dumb on purpose. "My older brother. He was coming home for vacation from college in England when the plane crashed."

"That's rough. I'm sorry."

He didn't acknowledge my sympathy. He didn't bother to ask me who I'd lost.

I told him anyway. "My father and mother were returning from an education conference in London. They were *both* on the plane."

No comment. He just wandered into my room and looked around like he was considering renting it for a homeless bag lady.

I found myself making excuses. "I really only just moved in. It'll be better when it's fixed up." Although it galled me to defend a room I hated, I didn't want him to think this was how I usually lived.

He shrugged and sat down on the Hide-A-Bed. He picked up the book on Shakespearean theaters and thumbed idly through it. I felt like he was reading my diary. I reached for the book. "That's for an English report."

He held on to it. "I'll bet going back to school was a hoot."

"I haven't gone back yet."

"Why not? It's two weeks since the plane crash."

Was today really the two-week anniversary of the crash? Sometimes it seemed like Mom and Dad had left yesterday. Other times it seemed like four hundred years ago. But I wasn't going to admit to this smart-aleck boy that my time sense was all messed up. I said, "I want to finish my English report before I go back to school."

"Yeah. Sure."

I didn't argue. It would only encourage him.

He didn't need any encouragement. He said with relish, "All the kids will stare at you like you're some kind of freak."

I insisted, "They won't!" But once he put the idea in my head, it was hard not to worry about it. I was an outsider to start with. The girls I hung around with in school were really Jill's friends, and Jill hadn't even called to see if I needed the homework assignments.

He just smiled, content that he'd scored a bull's-eye. I was glad of the distraction when Bathsheba came bounding in. She leapt up to her favorite spot on the Hide-A-Bed. Finding it taken, she sniffed delicately at the boy's hand. Then she jumped down and stalked out of the room.

To get back at him for the freak crack, I said, "Don't be too insulted. Bathsheba is very choosy about her friends."

"Your cat obviously smelled my dog on my hands. I dislike people assigning human feelings to animals."

I disliked him. And there was no reason to keep being polite to him. He was Alice's guest, not mine. I said, "I have to go feed the animals now. See you around." Then I headed for the back stairs. I wouldn't be able to hear the meeting down in the office. Why hadn't I thought of that before?

I couldn't have made it any clearer that he was most definitely not invited to accompany me. He didn't get the message. He followed me down the stairs, looked around, and asked, "Who's the vet?"

"My aunt." Maybe if I didn't give him more than two words at a time he'd go away.

"Is she any good?"

"Yes." I turned my back on him, opened Rex's cage, and checked his food bowl. Had he eaten a little?

"She hasn't done much for that dog. He's a miserable specimen."

That did it. "Don't you dare call Rex names! Of course he's miserable. The people he loved went away and left him. He's so heartbroken he can't even eat. He's dying of grief. But you can't understand that."

"Maybe I can."

He said it so low that I almost didn't catch it. When I did, I felt terrible. Because he was obnoxious, I'd forgotten that he was in the same boat as Rex—and me.

We stood there with what I'd said hanging in the air

between us. Then he dug into his pocket and came up with a doggy treat. "Rex might eat this. My dog loves them."

He bent to offer Rex the treat. I bent to take it from him because Rex was more likely to eat from the hand of someone he knew.

Our heads banged together. I saw stars.

chapter
8

The stars faded as the sun rose. Rooji and I hurried from the bakeshop to the alehouse, buying bread, cheese, and beer for the actors' breakfast. We'd been hired as helpers by the Duke's Men, which Rooji said was the best acting company in London next to Cousin Will's.

Being helpers meant we ran the errands and did the fetching and carrying. There was plenty of that in a world without electricity or even running water. We were constantly being sent here or there by Master Greene, the company manager; by Master Bowen, the playwright; by Master Fletcher, who was in charge of the costumes; or by one of the actors who owned shares in the company. Even the boy actors found jobs for us to do. The only person who didn't keep us running was the duke, our patron. That was only because he was too grand to notice us. When the duke came to see a play, he sat in his special armchair right on the stage.

Rooji had said we were lucky acting wasn't respectable like being a tailor or silversmith. Your family had to pay for you to be an apprentice and learn those trades. Master Greene had taken us on without our paying anything. Of course, we didn't get paid either. We got food to eat, a *pallet* (straw mattress) to sleep on, and a chance to earn an occasional penny watching a nobleman's horse during a performance if we weren't needed backstage. Today we were sure to be needed because the duke was honoring the company by coming to see our new play.

Although the performance didn't start until the afternoon, the theater was already humming with activity when we got back with the food. The playwright and the actor who played the king had their heads together over some new lines for the king's speech about the witch. Other actors were rehearsing dueling and death scenes. Meanwhile, the boy who played the queen complained that his gown was too long, and Master Fletcher demanded to know who had borrowed the furred cloak and spilled wine on it. Master Greene was shouting them all down in a voice like a trumpet. Rooji asked, "Is it not exciting?" I agreed that it was.

Everyone sat down where they were to eat. The food we'd brought had to last us until dinner after the performance. Dinner was the big meal of the day with meat, fowl, fish, and a sweet afterward. Now the company passed the bread and cheese around quickly. First Master Greene, Master Bowen, and Master Fletcher hacked off large chunks with the knives that everyone carried for the purpose. Next the actors cut off their pieces. Then we less important people shared what was left. I cut mine with the little knife I kept in the leather case attached to my belt.

After we ate, Master Fletcher sent me backstage to sponge the stains out of the furred cloak. I liked working with the costumes. The kings' and queens' robes were real silk, satin, or velvet. They were trimmed with gold spangles or silver lace. On an impulse, I draped myself in a brilliant yellow satin robe. It made me feel daring and powerful.

Hearing a commotion out front, I hurriedly hung the robe back on its peg and ran out to see what was happening. The actors were clustered at the front of the stage looking down into the pit. The boy who played the queen was lying on the rushes. He was clutching his leg and moaning.

Rooji told me, "He tripped over his gown and fell off the stage."

Master Greene came striding angrily across the stage. He shouted at the boy actor, "Get up, you lazy rapscallion!" The boy moaned that his leg was broken. Master Greene threatened to hoist him up by the scruff of his dirty neck. The boy lay there cringing. Finally, Master Greene sent for an *apothecary* (herb seller and bonesetter), vowing to take the cost out of the boy's hide if he were not truly injured.

The apothecary said the boy's ankle was sprained. He had to rest it for a week. Master Greene, cursing knaves who fell on the day the duke was coming, promoted the boy playing the lady-in-waiting to the queen's role. Which left him without a lady-in-waiting. He glared at Rooji and me. "It needs be one of you."

Rooji grabbed my hand so hard that I thought I'd need the bonesetter, too. Master Greene looked us over like a shopper deciding between two limp heads of lettuce. He pointed to me and ordered, "Get your costume from Master Fletcher." He stalked off before I could even think of arguing.

Rooji looked like she'd been kicked in the stomach, but she managed a brave smile. "The lady-in-waiting role is short enough for you to learn by this afternoon. And it has a poetic speech to show off your acting talent." In spite of her effort to be a good loser, a tear trickled down her cheek.

"The role would show off *your* acting talent. I'm no actor. We'll have to ask Master Greene to change his mind and give you the part."

She shook her head. "We must accept his decision."

I figured she was scared. Master Greene had a temper like fireworks waiting for a match. I tried to soothe her. "He'll probably yell at us for bothering him, but once he sees you act he'll be glad we did. We'll ask him to let you audition. You know, act a part for him. Maybe that princess speech."

"He is our master. We must be content that he knows what is best."

"How can he know when he's never seen you act?"

She just shook her head again. Why was she being so stubborn?

There wasn't time to stand and argue with her. I grabbed her arm and pulled her across the stage. She hung back. I pulled harder.

I was so intent on dragging Rooji to Master Greene's office that I didn't see him coming toward us. His hands grabbed my shoulders, and he shook me so hard that I nearly got whiplash. He thundered, "Cease your brawling! Or I will throw you into the gutter to starve."

Master Greene's voice could drown out a rock group, but Rooji managed to make herself heard over it. "Please, kind master," she begged, "do not throw us out. We were not brawling."

"Not brawling? Ha! Pray tell, what were you doing? Dancing?"

Rooji stammered, "Lee was trying to get me to ask you for the lady-in-waiting role."

He demanded, "Why should you have the role?"

She looked terrified. "Because I want to be an actor more than anything in the world."

He gave her his examining-a-limp-lettuce look. "Then act!"

Instead of the princess speech, Rooji acted out a scene in which she begged Master Greene for the lady-in-waiting role and he began by being angry and ended up giving it to her. She mimicked his voice and gestures so perfectly that I had to hide my smiles behind my hand.

"Enough! I have no time for this foolery." He gave her a shove. "Go get your costume. I expect you to know your lines in one hour."

As I helped Rooji into a red velvet robe, Master Fletcher spotted me. He sent me to the silversmith's shop to make sure that the duke's cup would be delivered before the play. Master Fletcher had ordered a real silver cup for the poison scene. It would be presented to the duke as a souvenir after the performance. He warned me, "Mind you do not leave the shop until you see the cup on its way."

Promising Rooji I'd be back in time to see her act, I set

off for Silversmith's Lane. It was about an hour's walk across London Bridge into the center of town. When I got there, the silversmith said the cup was ready. He said he'd send it as soon as his journeyman returned from another errand. Since I'd been told to wait until the cup was on its way, I squatted down on my heels and waited. And waited and waited.

As I watched the silversmith engrave a design on a silver ring, it occurred to me that Ned's father was a silversmith, too. His shop was probably nearby. Maybe I could find Ned and tell him that Rooji (Robin to him) was acting her (his) first role today. It would be great if Ned could come back with me to see her act. I asked the silversmith if he knew Ned. He said he didn't. He told me to go look for my friend and get out from under his feet.

I asked for Ned in the shops up and down Silversmith's Lane. Unfortunately, Ned was a common name and half the 'prentices in London seemed to have dark curly hair and wear blue doublets. It might have helped if I knew Ned's father's name. But I didn't.

Someone told me to try Jeweler's Lane where there were also some silversmiths. But I didn't have time. Master Fletcher would be furious if I wasn't back at the theater to help the actors dress. And Rooji's part was in the first act. I couldn't miss that. I ran back to the shop to check on the cup.

The journeyman still hadn't returned. When I told the silversmith I had to get back to the theater, he said, "Go with an easy mind. I will send the cup soon."

I wasn't buying that. "Why must we wait for your journeyman? The cup isn't very big. I can take it back with me now."

The silversmith said he couldn't be responsible if I lost it. I said I'd be careful and it would save him the trouble of delivering it. He kept worrying about me losing the cup. I argued that he trusted his journeyman not to lose it. He said the journeyman was big and powerful. I didn't see what that had to do with it. I said I'd put the cup inside my doublet so it couldn't possibly fall out.

In the end, because it was getting so late, he reluctantly wrapped the cup in a piece of cloth and gave it to me. Turning my back modestly, I buttoned it into my doublet. I thanked him and ran out.

My doublet fit tightly and the front was stiffly padded. The padding was good for hiding that I was a girl, but it pressed the cup handle into my stomach. Every step I took pushed the handle deeper into me. By the time I'd gone a few blocks, I felt like someone was driving a sword through me. I had to get the cup out of there.

I couldn't very well undo my clothes in the middle of a busy street. I turned down the first quiet alley and then into a deserted dead end between two rows of houses. After a quick look around to make sure I was alone, I opened my doublet and pulled the cup out. What a relief!

That was my first chance to really look at the cup. It was a lovely thing: about six inches tall with two handles shaped like lions' heads and the duke's crest engraved on the front. One of the lion's heads had been digging into me.

As I admired the cup, I sensed somebody watching me. I looked up and saw two burly men strolling down the alley toward me. It suddenly dawned on me what the silversmith had meant by my losing the cup. I thought of the knife in my belt. But I hadn't a chance against those two gorillas. I considered throwing the cup down and dashing past them when they stopped to pick it up. But the cup was my responsibility. I couldn't bring myself to sacrifice it.

The men were getting nearer. They weren't hurrying. I was trapped in a dead end. They were sure they had me. One of them was smiling—not a friendly smile. I stuffed the cup back inside my doublet (ouch!) and looked around frantically for a way out. The only possibility was a space about a foot and a half wide between two of the houses. It was a tight fit, and there was no way of knowing if it went anywhere.

I sprinted toward it. As soon as I made my move, the men broke into a run as well. Their footsteps pounded behind me as I reached the opening. Their hands grabbed at me as I squirmed in sideways. It was like being in a tunnel in a horror movie. The kind where the walls move together to trap the hero. For a second, I panicked. Then I saw a faint light at the end of the tunnel.

I wriggled toward the light. The cup, which had hurt my stomach when I walked in the street, was torture as I squirmed between wooden walls so close together that there was hardly room to breathe. About halfway through I banged my head on a low beam. I could feel blood trickling down my forehead. But the men were too heavy to come in after me. I'd outwitted them. The cup was safe.

The first thing I did when I finally emerged into an open yard was to pull the cup out and see that it wasn't dented or scratched. As I examined it, someone yelled, "Stop, thief!"

Startled, I looked around for the men who had tried to rob me. They were nowhere in sight, but a tall man in a silversmith's apron grabbed my shoulder and ordered, "Give me back my cup, thief."

He tried to pry the cup out of my hands. I hung on for dear life. I don't know what would have happened if Ned hadn't come running out of the shop shouting, "Father, stop! That is my friend Lee."

Things sorted themselves out quickly after that. When I explained what had happened, Ned's father said that with all the *footpads* (muggers) about, valuables should not be trusted to lads. He sent a strong helper armed with a *cudgel* (heavy stick) to deliver the cup to Master Fletcher. Then he told Ned to tend the cut on my forehead lest it fester.

I sat on a stool in the shop while Ned poured wine into the cut. It stung and dripped down my face. I licked the drops off my dry lips. It was refreshing. I opened my mouth for more.

Ned said, "For a little lad, you have a brave heart. Many bigger and stronger than you would have handed over the cup."

Me brave? That was a new thought. If someone had asked me a few hours (or centuries?) ago, I'd have described myself as shy and timid. But shy, timid girls don't outwit footpads and save the duke's cup. If I was brave and adventurous here . . .

Here. As Shakespeare said: There's the rub. I shook my head—which was a mistake. The wine was making me woozy. And talkative. I blurted out, "I don't think being brave here counts."

"Counts for what?"

That was a complicated problem. I tried to puzzle it out. "If this world is a place I escape to when my own world is too much to bear, does what I do here count? But if I can do it here . . ."

Ned shushed me. "You talk wildly because the blow on your head has disturbed the balance of humors in your body and addled your wits. Your wits will return when the wine overcomes the poisons in your wound."

Then he poured so much wine onto my head that it ran into my eyes and got up my nose. I coughed and sputtered.

chapter
9

S puttering, I pulled off the wet handkerchief that was plastered to my forehead and dripping water into my eyes and nose. The boy from the relatives' meeting said, "Welcome back to the land of the living. We didn't bang heads that hard, but I had to scrape you up off the floor." He took back his handkerchief and made a production of wringing it out over Rex's water bowl. "This was the only water I could find when you passed out. It's clean—if you don't count dog spit."

If he was trying to freak me out, he was wasting his time. I was already totally freaked out by finding myself back in a world where Mom and Dad had abandoned me, where Alice didn't care how awful I felt, and where the house was full of people acting as if they could change the horrible things that had happened.

I couldn't stand being here. I had to get away. I leapt to my feet as if someone had thrown a switch in my body. My legs carried me across the room, out the office door, into the street, and up the hill toward the park at a dead run. I didn't slow down until I reached the paved road that ran through the park. Then I stopped running as suddenly as I'd started. I stood in the middle of the road and tried to figure out what I was doing there.

The road was crowded with Sunday joggers and bikers. A biker in a neon spandex suit yelled at me to get the blankety-blank out of the way. A jogger pushing her baby in a three-wheeled contraption said the same thing more politely. I couldn't move. I didn't know where to go. I didn't know where I wanted to go.

A hand pulled me off the roadway onto the grass. The obnoxious boy had followed me. I cried, "Leave me alone!"

"So you can throw yourself under a bike or something? I sure don't want the job, but somebody's got to look out for you. You ran out of the house like a crazy woman."

He had a talent for saying the most upsetting thing possible. I insisted, "I'm not crazy! I just needed some fresh air." But once he made me think about it, I couldn't shake the feeling that running away like that was kind of peculiar.

He rubbed it in. "Face it. The plane crash made us all crazy."

Could he be right? I'd read about people going out of their minds from shock. Could my trips to the past be a crazy delusion? But I'd also read about time travel. Just a few weeks ago, I'd seen a magazine article where scientists predicted we'd have time travel in a hundred years. If it could happen in a hundred years, why not now? I said, "Speak for yourself, John."

"Brian."

"I was quoting from a poem."

"I hate poetry."

I didn't care what he hated. And I didn't care what he said. I wasn't crazy. I hadn't imagined Rooji and Ned and the Duke's Men. I wouldn't let him convince me that I had. I sat down in the grass and started looking for a four-leaf clover. Maybe if I found one it would take me back to the theater in time to see Rooji act.

Brian plopped down next to me. "What's your name?"

I was trying to ignore him, but it's hard not to answer a direct question. I muttered, "Lisa Barnett."

"So, Lisa, aren't you going to ask me what crazy things I do?"

"No." I moved to a new patch of grass. He followed me, sitting exactly where I'd intended to look. Exasperated, I said, "You're not crazy. You're just terribly annoying. And don't tell me you were all sweetness and light before."

"Of course I wasn't. When people go crazy, they don't go out of their minds. They go further into them."

Now what was that supposed to mean? I refused to give him the satisfaction of asking.

He told me anyway. "Take my father. He was always an organizer. When he flipped out, he went organization crazy. This relatives' group is just part of it. He's organizing letter-writing campaigns and protests and marches."

I couldn't resist saying, "I guess when you flipped out you got even more obnoxious."

He grinned like I'd paid him a compliment. "Let's say I always liked getting a rise out of people, so I do it more now. How has going crazy affected you? I mean, besides becoming fascinated by grass?"

I refused to let him get a rise out of me. I said calmly, "This is the most ridiculous conversation I've ever heard. For your information, I am not crazy and I am not fascinated by grass. I'm looking for a four-leaf clover." Then I stood up and brushed off my jeans. "However, it doesn't seem like I'm going to find one, and I have to get back now."

I headed against the stream of joggers and bikers, looking for where I'd come into the park. He followed me saying, "If you go against the traffic, you'll get knocked over."

A speeding biker proved his point by missing me by inches. I stepped out of the way, trying to decide what to do. "I came in back there. If I go out a different way, I'll end up wandering through the wilds of Brooklyn." I felt lost enough without that.

"This road makes a circle through the park. You could follow it around to where you came in."

I hesitated. I really didn't want to go back. The meeting would still be going strong. "Maybe I will. It's a nice day for a walk."

"Right. It's only four miles around."

Although I didn't actually remember it, I must have walked most of the distance from Stratford to London. That was eighty miles as the crow flies and longer by the twisting roads of the sixteenth century. Next to that, four miles around the park was nothing. I said, "I think I can manage it," and set off at a good pace. Glancing back over my shoulder, I added, "Unless it's too much for you."

Brian caught up with me, stayed by my side for a second, then pulled a step ahead of me. When I took an extra step to catch up with him, he took one more to keep in front. We were walking at the same speed, but he seemed to be going faster because he was a step ahead. It was very annoying. I caught up and passed him. I didn't keep the lead for long. A few seconds later he was in front again.

Filled with the determination that had outwitted the footpads and saved the duke's cup, I passed him again. Now we were jogging instead of walking. After a few more exchanges of the lead we were jogging fast. Before long we were running. Then running fast. Brian's long legs gave him a big advantage in a flat-out run. So I slowed down, forcing him to cut his pace to keep a single step in front of me. When we were down to a walk, I passed him.

It was a strange race that nobody could win. At least, it seemed like nobody could win until he passed me for the umpteenth time and suddenly sprinted down a side path and out of the park. Too late, I saw that we'd come full circle. There was nothing I could do but follow him out of the park.

He strolled along with his hands in his pockets and a smug look on his face. Then he said, "Our little walk made me thirsty. Want a soda?"

"I don't have any money with me."

"I'll treat you."

The unexpected offer was tempting. I didn't want to go back to Alice's house while the meeting was still going on. Actually, I never wanted to go back. And I was thirsty. "Just lend me some money. I'll pay you back when I get my allowance."

"Suit yourself. We'll go to Carr's. They make real whipped cream so thick you can pick it up by the handful."

He'd probably do exactly that just to gross me out. Then something else occurred to me. "How come you know the neighborhood so well?"

"My parents own a brownstone down that block. A house like your aunt's except the top floor isn't a separate apartment. We live in the whole thing."

"If you have all that room, why did your father ask my aunt to have the meeting at her house?"

Brian didn't answer.

He was the most annoying person. One minute he was offering to treat me to a soda, the next he wouldn't answer a perfectly reasonable question. I had a right to know why his father had inflicted the meeting on me. I insisted, "The meeting was your father's idea. Why wasn't it in your house?"

"If you must know, my mother refuses to see anyone since my brother was killed. She won't go out of the house, and she won't let people in. Does that answer your question? Does that make you happy?"

It answered my question, but it didn't make me happy. That was the second time I'd hurt him without meaning to. I muttered, "I'm sorry."

"Fat lot of good your being sorry does."

He didn't have to be so nasty about it. Or maybe he did. Maybe being obnoxious was the only way he knew how to deal with hurting. Like all I knew was to crawl into myself and clam up.

We didn't say another word until we got to Carr's. The place was fixed up like a 1940s soda shop with World War II posters on the walls and an old jukebox playing "swing" records. We sat on wrought-iron chairs at a round marble-topped table. Brian ordered an all-chocolate ice-cream soda

with extra whipped cream. I'd planned to have a Coke, but I changed my mind at the last minute and said I'd have the same.

My soda came in a glass so tall that I had to stand up to get my mouth on the straw. I scarfed it down, alternating spoonfuls of chocolate ice cream and whipped cream with gulps of chocolate soda. I hardly stopped for breath until my glass was half empty.

"Good, huh?"

I was embarrassed to be caught gobbling like I hadn't tasted food in weeks. In a way, I hadn't. I had had no appetite, and when I did eat the food tasted like cardboard. Now the sweetness in my mouth made me greedy and I couldn't get enough. I forced myself to put my spoon down and look around. "I like the way this place is fixed up."

Brian used two fingers to scoop a blob of whipped cream off the rim of his glass. He popped it into his mouth and licked his fingers. I needn't have worried about looking like a pig; next to him I was Miss Manners. He said, "I came here with my grandfather for lunch. Grampa was a teenager in the forties, and he said that being here was like going back in time."

His last words sent a shiver down my spine. Although I knew I shouldn't open the subject, I couldn't resist. I said casually, "I read this article about time travel. I think it was in the *Times* science section. It said that time travel is theoretically possible. It might be practical in as little as a hundred years. Isn't that interesting?"

To my surprise, Brian pounced on the idea like a cat on a mouse. "Interesting! People have been fascinated by the idea of time travel practically since time began and you make it sound like a trip to the mall. Don't you have any imagination? Imagine being able to go back into the past and see Washington cross the Delaware or Babe Ruth hit his seven-hundredth home run."

He was such a smug know-it-all that I had to stuff my mouth with ice cream to keep from telling him that I didn't have to *imagine* going back into the past. But I knew he'd never believe me. I know how I'd have reacted a few weeks ago if someone told me she'd been in sixteenth-century London with Shakespeare's cousin.

He slurped more soda and said, "It'd be fun to watch one of those battles with knights in armor fighting on horse-back."

"You couldn't just stand and watch. If you showed up in the middle of a battle, you'd end up stuck on somebody's lance like a shish kabob. You'd have to hide or—better still—get some knight to take you on as a squire and then fight on his side."

"What makes you think it would work that way?"

Too bad I couldn't tell him how I *knew* it worked that way. "I read a lot of books. Stories about long ago."

"Oh, stories." He dismissed them with a shrug. "I'm interested in facts. Scientific facts."

I just spooned up more ice cream. I was getting the hang of being with him. The trick was to ignore him when he acted obnoxious.

It worked. He said, "It'd be even more fun to be part of the past. I'd know more than anyone else. I'd know what was going to happen."

"You'd know the things in history books, like who'd be elected president. But you wouldn't know who won that battle you were talking about unless it was a famous one you'd studied in school. You wouldn't know what was going to happen to the people you were with."

Brian didn't argue the point. He was looking thoughtfully at a World War II poster on the wall. The poster showed a battleship exploding in a red burst of fire. He said, "The shorter the time ago something happened, the more I'd know about it."

"I guess so." I didn't see what he was driving at.

"If it was only two weeks ago, I'd know what was going to happen."

I caught on. "Yes, but that's not . . ."

He broke in triumphantly, "So I could go back and stop it from happening. I could warn my brother not to take the plane."

"No, you couldn't! It doesn't work like that!" If it was possible, wouldn't I go back and save Mom and Dad?

Brian looked like I'd wakened him out of a wonderful dream. I tried to soften the blow. "I mean, time travel is just an idea we're playing with."

"Sure. We'd have to be crazy to take it seriously."

There didn't seem to be anything else to say. I picked up the check the waiter had left on the table and did the math in my head. "I owe you two dollars and sixty-two cents. That's three dollars and twelve cents with my share of the tip."

"Three dollars will do."

"I'll pay you back as soon as I get my allowance."

"Whenever."

"I guess I'll head back. The meeting must be over by now and my aunt will worry that I got lost or something."

chapter
10

Mom would have been worried sick if I left the house without letting her know and didn't come back for hours. Alice didn't care. When I apologized, saying I'd gone running in the park with Brian Gordon and we'd lost track of time, she just said, "It was a nice day for the park." She didn't even react when I told her we'd had huge chocolate ice-cream sodas afterward. She thinks chocolate is worse poison than sugar and won't let either of them in the house. But she acted like it was fine with her if I wrecked my body and made my face break out.

All she cared about was the relatives' group giving her the job of organizing a protest at the airline office. You'd think they'd elected her president of the United States the way she talked about it.

She said, "Lives are at stake. We have to demand that the airlines take stricter security measures. Those metal detectors are a joke. A child could get a bomb into Kennedy, and that's one of the best protected airports in the country. I shudder to think of the rest of the world. We must pressure the airlines to make real changes instead of handing out press releases saying how safe we are. If I can get enough people to show up at the airline office, they will have to listen to us. Especially if we have the protest while the crash is still in the public's mind. Some of the other relatives thought that two weeks from today was too soon to get a protest organized, but I convinced them I could do it."

Alice would have gone on about it all day if I'd given her any encouragement. She has no patience with polite conversation, but once she gets started on something she cares about, it's as if there's nothing else in the world. I said, "I guess it's worth trying." Then I told her I didn't remember if I'd closed Rex's cage before I went out. I said I'd better go check.

The cage was closed. When I opened it and petted Rex, he felt a little less limp under my hand. I looked around for Brian's doggie treat. It was gone. Either Brian never gave it to Rex, or Rex had eaten it. I tried a dog biscuit on him. Rex seemed to sniff it with more interest than the last time, but he didn't eat it. I left it in his cage.

When I came back upstairs, Alice was marching around the living room with the cordless phone glued to her ear. She left a trail of telephone books and scribbled notes behind her. I sprawled on the sofa while she called people to tell them about the protest. She emphasized how important it was to get a big turnout and begged them to spread the word. She asked them to make signs and armbands. She picked their brains about publicity and permits. I kept waiting for her to ask me to do something. I practiced a little speech in my head reminding her that she'd promised not to involve me in the relatives' group's doings. But she never asked.

There's nothing more boring than listening to someone else's phone conversations. I went to look for Bathsheba. I found her batting her catnip mouse across the bathroom floor. When I bent down to pet her, she made it clear that she wasn't in a people mood. I washed my hands and face and combed my hair. I considered taking a long hot bath, but that meant scrubbing the crud out of the tub first.

Alice was still jabbering away when I went back to the living room. She hadn't noticed that I'd left. She didn't notice that I was back. I went to my room and closed the door behind me—hard. The steady murmur of Alice's voice continued without a break. I plopped myself down in the lumpy armchair.

What an ugly room! It was the ugliest room I'd ever seen. I hated it. I jumped out of the chair, shoving it away from me. The chair hit the wall with a thud. Mom would have come in to find out what on earth I was doing. There was no reaction from Alice.

I threw myself onto the Hide-A-Bed and stared at the ugly cracked ceiling. I couldn't bear being in that horrible, suffocating room all alone. But there was no place to go and no one to turn to.

Suddenly, without a bump on the head or a four-leaf clover, I was in the dressing room of the theater. Rooji was lacing up her lady-in-waiting costume. I was so happy to be back with her that I didn't even wonder how I'd managed it. I laughed out of pure happiness.

Rooji said, "Do not laugh at me. My lines have flown out of my head. I cannot remember a word."

I said, "All actors have stage fright. You'll be fine when you step on stage. Did I tell you Ned is coming to see you act?"

"To see me disgrace myself."

"You'll be great. Everything will be great."

Master Greene shouted for me to help carry the duke's armchair onto the stage. Then I was so busy going down to the cellar for props and dashing back up to the musicians' gallery with new strings for the lute player that I didn't notice that we were late getting started.

Everything was ready. The musicians had already played two songs to entertain the audience that packed the pit and galleries. But the trumpet still hadn't signaled the start of the play. Peeking out at the audience in the hope of spotting Ned in the pit, I saw what was holding things up. The duke's armchair on the stage was empty.

The duke still hadn't arrived after the musicians played three more songs. Master Bowen, the playwright, said we would have trouble with the audience if we didn't start soon. Master Greene almost bit his head off. After that, nobody made any suggestions.

Rooji was getting so nervous that she was shaking. I patted her shoulder. "Relax. The duke probably got stuck at court. You can't just walk out on the queen, you know."

Finally, the stage door flew open and a splendid figure, accompanied by three gentlemen, strode majestically in. The actors' costumes looked like crepe paper next to the duke's gold-slashed doublet with diamond buttons, his embroidered cape and ostrich-plumed hat, his chains and pearls and brooches. I whispered to Rooji as we bowed low, "I told you everything would be fine."

I spoke too soon. The duke called Master Greene and Master Bowen over. Because the audience out front was whistling and stamping, we couldn't hear what the duke was saying to them. However, his face and gestures made it clear that he was very angry. Master Bowen turned pale.

Rooji whispered anxiously, "The duke's wrath affrights me."

The duke stopped talking. He turned on his high heel and marched back out the stage door. His gentlemen followed him.

Master Greene called the company together to tell us why the duke was angry. I strained my ears to hear. The audience was so noisy that I only caught a few words: "the lord chamberlain . . . witch's speech . . . treason."

I asked Rooji, "How can the duke call the new play treason? Treason means overthrowing the government. Besides, he hasn't seen the play yet."

"The duke's agent saw yesterday's rehearsal and reported that Master Bowen had changed the speech about the witch after the lord chamberlain's office approved the play. Now the witch can be taken to mean the queen. It is treason to criticize the queen. If we perform the play, the lord chamberlain will shut down our theater and imprison Master Bowen. And I'll never get a chance to act." She began to cry.

I tried to think of something to comfort her. The audience was making so much noise that I couldn't think.

The audience yelled and stamped. Stamp! Bang! Knock! Knock!

———

Alice was knocking on the door of my room. Angry at her dragging me back, I pretended I was napping and didn't hear her. At least she wouldn't come into my room without permission. She has this thing about people needing their own space. I held my breath until I heard her walk away. Then I lay on the Hide-A-Bed and tried to figure out a way to get back to Rooji. I couldn't leave her alone in her misery.

There had to be a key. I racked my brain. I couldn't find any connection between the Shakespeare garden, the living room picture, banging my head in the office, and this last switch. Except Alice. Alice had been in the Shakespeare garden, and the other switches happened in her house. I'd have to sound her out without telling her why I was asking.

Alice wasn't in the living room. She wasn't in the kitchen, the bathroom, or her bedroom. She'd gone off and left me. I didn't know where or for how long. She hadn't bothered to leave me a note.

I wandered through the empty rooms, too fidgety to sit still, and finally stopped in front of the refrigerator. I wasn't really hungry, but eating is something to do and food is company. I could have gone for a thick pastrami sandwich on bakery rye, but Alice won't have any kind of meat in the house. Not even chicken or fish. I scrounged behind the leftover tofu and vegiburger. There was nothing any normal person would put in her mouth unless she was starving to death.

A voice behind me said, "Before I went down to the office I knocked on your door to suggest phoning for pizza."

"No pizza!" I could never forget that I was stuffing myself with pepperoni pizza while Mom and Dad's plane was blowing up. "I mean, no thanks."

"Because pizza is fast food, most people don't realize that it is nourishing. Especially topped with vegetables. There's a place on Seventh Avenue that makes a great zucchini and eggplant pizza."

I'd never eat pizza again if I lived to be a hundred. "I'm not hungry. That ice-cream soda filled me up."

"Then I'll just finish the vegiburger. Why don't you keep me company while I eat? It will give us a chance to talk."

When a grown-up (even Alice) wants to talk, you can bet she has something on her mind that you don't want to hear. This wasn't the time to feel her out for a clue to getting back to Rooji. When you're on the spot, the best way to get off it is to put the other person there. I said quickly, "Maybe we could talk about my allowance. I had to borrow money from Brian for the soda today. I should pay him back."

It worked. She asked, "Why didn't you say something sooner?" like it was my responsibility. She went to the COFFEE canister she used for loose change and bills. "How much allowance do you usually get?"

"Thirty dollars. But that also covers school money. I guess I won't need that much this week."

In trying to be fair, I'd put my foot squarely in it. She held out three tens saying, "Going back to school is one of the things I wanted to talk to you about."

I didn't want to talk about it. Not after Brian's saying I'd be treated like a freak. I didn't answer or take the money.

She cleared her throat. "Is there something bothering you about going back to school?"

I stared at the floor.

"Fine! Don't tell me. Don't talk to me at all. I'm sick and

· 68 ·

tired of trying to drag two civil words out of you. Go back to school and don't bother me."

So much for her bending over backward to be kind and understanding. In a way, it was a relief to know how she really felt. It freed me to feel the way I felt about her. "When are you making me go back?"

"Tomorrow morning."

"All right. I'll go. You're my guardian, and I have to do what you say." I knew she hated when I talked like that. I waited for the throat clearing. When it didn't come, I asked, "Now can I have your permission to go pay Brian back?"

She held out the money. I grabbed it and ran out of the house. I forgot that I didn't know where Brian lived. I had to go back to get his address from Alice. She gave it to me without comment.

Although I could pay him back anytime, I was in a strange hurry to get to Brian's house. I certainly wasn't running to see him because I liked him. He got on my nerves. I alternated between wanting to tell him off and being guilty for hurting his feelings. But since the plane crash I seemed to have forgotten how to do ordinary things with ordinary people. Because Brian was in the same boat, we had to stick together.

There was no answer when I rang the bell, although there was a light in the front room. Maybe they hadn't heard. Maybe they were eating dinner and didn't want to be disturbed. Maybe I should go away.

Go where? I put my finger on the bell and pressed hard.

Finally, the door opened and Brian stepped out onto the stoop. He stood there barefoot, his body blocking the door.

I said, "I came to pay you back," and held out a ten-dollar bill to prove it.

"Forget it."

"No. It was a loan. Take it."

"I don't have change."

"You can give me the change another time."

"Then I'd owe you seven dollars instead of your owing me three. That's dumb."

It had been dumb of me to come. Dumber to think that we could help each other. Look how he was guarding the door. You'd think I was trying to steal the TV and stereo.

Then I remembered his mother hiding in the house. I said, "I'm going to buy a candy bar at the newsstand. I'll change the ten there. Why don't you come along so I can pay you back?"

He went inside to get his sneakers, closing the door behind him. He left me standing on the stoop so long I started thinking it was a trick to get rid of me. When he finally came out, we walked to the newsstand without talking.

I bought my candy and handed him his three dollars. He stuck the money in his pocket and asked, "Why did you really drag me out here?"

I wished I hadn't. "I told you, to pay you back. Now forget it, will you?"

That was like asking a dog to forget a juicy bone, like asking someone who had picked the right numbers to forget his lottery ticket. Brian nagged me to tell him what was so important that I came to his house and dragged him away from his dinner. I said I hadn't known he was eating. I told him to go home and finish. I said I was headed for my own dinner and started walking back toward Alice's house.

He followed me, nagging all the way. Finally he said, "It's about what we were discussing in Carr's, isn't it?"

I'd been walking fast to discourage him. I slowed down and asked cautiously, "What makes you think that?"

"So that *is* it! I knew you were hiding something. What is it?"

"You wouldn't believe me if I told you."

"Probably not."

He was trying to goad me into telling him. It worked. I guess I'd intended to tell him all along. I had to confide in someone. I sat down on Alice's stoop and started with meeting Rooji again in Stratford. I went through the story of our running away to London and joining the Duke's Men, right up to the duke's calling the new play treason and Rooji being afraid the lord chamberlain would close the company down and she wouldn't be able to act.

When I finished, Brian didn't say I was crazy. He didn't accuse me of putting him on. He nodded as if he'd known all along it was something like that. Then he started asking questions. "After we banged heads, you only passed out for a few minutes. But the way you tell it, you had time to walk across London, wait at the silversmith's, and outwit the muggers. How could that be?"

Trust Brian to complicate things. I hadn't thought of the time difference. Even though the same thing happened when I was hypnotized by the picture over the sofa. From the look of my room after Alice finished cleaning it up, she couldn't have spent more than ten minutes in there. But I'd had time to wander through London with Rooji, meet Ned, and see a play. I searched for some kind of reasonable answer. "Who said time has to move at the same rate in the past and present?"

Brian seemed to accept that. But he refused to leave well enough alone. "How do you know all about joining the Duke's Men if you weren't actually there? And doesn't Rooji miss you when you're in the present?"

I demanded, "Are you going to sit here asking me impossible questions, or are you going to help me get back to Rooji?"

"I'm going to help you get back to Rooji." He said it so sweetly that I got suspicious. Before I could figure out what he was up to, he said, "The first thing we'll do is look up what happened to the Duke's Men. Meet me at the library tomorrow afternoon."

"My aunt is making me go back to school tomorrow."

"After school. Three thirty."

His missing the chance for a smart-aleck comment about school made me even more suspicious. And I didn't see how researching the Duke's Men would get me back to Rooji. But I didn't have a better idea. "Make it four o'clock. I don't know how long it will take me to get back from Manhattan."

chapter
11

School was exhausting. I don't know if everyone really was staring at me. I felt as if they were, which was just as bad. People I hardly knew came up to me and told me they were sorry about my parents. I didn't know what to answer. I just wished they'd leave me alone.

The girls I ate lunch with told me how awful they felt. I didn't know what to say to them either, so I asked about the work I'd missed. Jill said she had called to give me the assignments. Melinda said she'd called, too, which surprised me. They had both left messages on the answering machine in my old apartment.

Jill said she understood I was too upset to call back. But I could see she was hurt. I had to explain that I never got her call because I was living with my aunt in Brooklyn. She asked, "Why didn't your aunt change the answering machine message to tell people where you were?"

"Alice doesn't think about things like that." I tried to sound like Alice's carelessness didn't bother me so Jill wouldn't start asking questions. Jill loves gossip. Luckily, she was being careful of my feelings because of Mom and Dad. She didn't try to get the lowdown on Alice. Instead she and Melinda fell all over themselves to catch me up on my schoolwork. I just wished they wouldn't try so hard.

When school was finally over, I got on the wrong train to Brooklyn. By the time I discovered my mistake, doubled back, and found the right train, I was really dragging. It was a quarter after four when I finally climbed up the subway stairs. Too late to stop at the house to drop my schoolbooks or to look in on Rex. I had to go straight to the library to meet Brian.

Brian got a librarian to help us. She found information on how playwrights in Shakespeare's time sneaked criticism of the government into their plays. I began to suspect that Master Bowen had done it on purpose. The librarian tried to find out what had happened to the Duke's Men. She couldn't discover any reference to them at all. I was ready to give up. I hadn't seen the point of going to the library in the first place. But Brian insisted that we had to know. The librarian tried just one more place. Then one more. Finally, she ran out of places to try.

As we left the library, Brian looked so glum that I said, "The librarian did her best."

"What difference does that make? We still don't know if the theater was closed down or if the playwright went to prison." He glared at me like it was my fault. Like he was the one trying to get back to the past and I was stopping him.

I opened my mouth to ask him what good knowing what happened would do. Then I shut it again. Reasoning with Brian was a waste of energy, and I had no energy to spare. My schoolbooks were growing heavier by the minute, and I was getting more and more tired. I felt like a car tire going flat. I just wanted to plop into bed and sleep.

Although it was only a few blocks from the library to Alice's house, the distance loomed in front of me like the marathon. I dragged myself across Flatbush Avenue. Brian followed me, insisting, "We're missing something. There has to be a way. There has to be."

The light turned red, trapping us on the island in the middle of the street. I leaned against the lamppost and almost fell asleep standing up. Brian stood next to me demanding, "How did you get back into the past before?" It was worse than a mosquito buzzing in my ear and keeping me awake. He kept asking, "How did you do it? How?"

●━●━●

"How do we tell the audience there will be no performance today?" Rooji asked anxiously.

I wanted to shout to Brian, "This is how I do it!"

Rooji added, "Or any day. Master Bowen will be called by the lord chamberlain's office to prove he meant no treason. Until he is cleared—if he is cleared—we cannot perform. Who knows when I will have another chance to act."

I comforted her, "I'm sure Master Bowen will talk his way out of it. And Master Greene is bound to give you another role later on."

Master Greene called the company together and explained what to do when he announced that the play was canceled. He organized us like we were soldiers going into battle and he was our general. He posted the three huskiest actors at the strongbox to refund money. The boy actors, Rooji, and I were sent onstage to shout, "Move to the exits," while the other actors herded the audience out of the pit and galleries.

When we were all in position, Master Greene stepped to the front of the stage and made the announcement. His booming voice carried through the theater like he'd just invented the microphone.

There was a shocked silence. Then an angry growl. Then the men and boys in the pit swarmed onto the stage, cursing and screaming and tearing up anything they could get their hands on. Hunks of scenery went flying in every direction as the mob rushed at us like a herd of stampeding buffalo.

The boy actors turned and fled. Rooji stood her ground shouting, "Move to the exits." At least, that's what I think she was shouting. I couldn't hear her over the fury of the crowd. I yelled, "Let's get out of here," and reached for her hand to pull her backstage to safety. It was too late. We were separated. Rooji was swallowed up by the mob while I was swept to the front of the stage.

I teetered on the edge and almost tumbled into the pit. Then a hand grabbed my shoulder and steadied me. "Ned!" I exclaimed. "Am I glad to see you."

<hr />

Brian asked, "What did you call me? Ed?"

I wanted to call him a lot of names for dragging me back. I shook his hand off my shoulder.

"Some gratitude. Next time I'll let you walk out into the traffic and get yourself killed."

"I wasn't walking into the traffic. I was . . ."

He caught on immediately. His face lit up. He was pleasant looking when he wasn't sulking or scowling. "You were back there! That's why you looked like you were sleep-walking." When I nodded, he asked eagerly, "How did you do it? What is the secret of time travel?"

"I don't know any secret. It just happens."

"You must have some idea."

"Don't you think I've tried to figure it out? I thought it might have something to do with Alice, but she wasn't around this time. So I haven't a clue."

"That's because you haven't gone about it systematically." He pulled me to a bench and opened his notebook. "We'll make a list."

His superior tone annoyed me, but I was ready to try anything that might get me back to Rooji. I was worried about her. That mob was out for blood.

Brian made three lists. First he listed the times I went into the past: where I was, who was there, how I felt, and so on. Then he did the same for returning to the present. The third list was the ways I'd tried to get back to the past: reading by candlelight, staring at the picture in the living room, trying to hypnotize myself, and so on. He asked me a thousand questions and wrote down all my answers.

Finally he shut his notebook and stood up. "I'll go over all this and see if I can find a pattern. I'll let you know if I do." He started to walk away.

"Wait. I wanted to ask you. What happened to the doggie treat you tried to give Rex? After we bumped heads, did you take it back?"

"No. Why?"

"It wasn't in Rex's cage, so he must've eaten it."

"Unless it's lying on the floor somewhere."

Trust Brian to think of that. I said, "The 'scientifically balanced diet' Alice gives Rex is as tempting as the vegetarian glop she gives me. No wonder Rex won't touch it. But if he ate the doggie treat, he might eat hamburger. Now that I have money again, I'm going to buy him some."

After a detour to a butcher shop on Seventh Avenue, I finally got back to the house and dropped my books. I ran straight down to the office with the hamburger. There was still a patient in the waiting room. A brightly colored parrot perched on his owner's shoulder like a large ornament. I was glad that Alice was still busy. I was afraid she wouldn't let me try the hamburger on Rex.

I opened Rex's cage and stroked his head with one hand. With my other hand I held a little raw hamburger under his nose so he could smell it. I held the meat there until my arm ached.

Suddenly his tongue lapped my palm. The meat was gone! I put a little more on my hand and tried again. Slowly, Rex ate it all.

I was so happy that I did a hop-skip-twirl of joy—and bumped smack into Alice.

She must have been standing watching me. All her talk about giving other people space didn't stop her from spying. Angry and embarrassed, I muttered something about not wanting to forget my jazz exercise routines.

She didn't buy it. She grabbed my hands and danced me around the room singing, "Hallelujah! Hallelujah!" Her noisy carrying-on started Rex barking. "Do you hear that?" she demanded. "Rex is going to be all right. And you did it!" She pretended to pin a medal on my shirt. Then she kissed me on both cheeks the way French generals do in movies. It was so silly that I couldn't help giggling. She was really weird, but at that moment I liked it.

Of course, she couldn't leave me feeling good. She had to push it. She had to say that two great things had just happened. Rex was one, and the guy with the parrot was the other. The parrot guy's brother was a cameraman for Channel 5 News. If she could produce a big crowd for the protest, he'd see that it got TV coverage.

She gave me an earnest look. "I know you said you didn't want to get involved and you don't have to. But TV publicity would make the airlines listen. The problem is that we won't get the publicity unless we get the crowd. After a tragedy, people ask what they can do to help. If your friends ask, would you tell them to spread the word about the protest?"

There was no way to say "No." I promised, "If they ask what they can do, I'll mention the protest." Luckily, so far nobody had asked.

"Are you sure? You can refuse if you want."

Like heck I could. "I don't mind as long as I don't have to go to the protest myself."

chapter
12

A lice threw herself into organizing the protest like there was no tomorrow. Whenever she wasn't down in the office catching up on her work, she was busy with the protest. Which was fine with me. It was easier to live with her if I didn't see her too much.

For someone who didn't get around to buying milk or doing the laundry until we were dying of thirst and going naked, Alice was surprisingly efficient when it came to the protest. Master Greene would have approved of the way she took charge. She got a permit. She made signs and badgered the neighborhood stores into putting them in their windows. She convinced the local newspaper to announce the event and kept after the parrot man's brother. She set up an each-one-reach-one chain, phoning everyone she'd ever met and persuading that person to call one more person and get that person to call one more and so on.

Meanwhile, I went to school, turned in my English report, caught up on the assignments I'd missed, coaxed Rex into eating, and even read the new Mary Higgins Clark mystery. I did all the normal things, but I didn't feel normal. I felt like I was seeing everything from a distance. Like I was floating in a bubble a few feet off the ground. Even my worry about Rooji and my need to get back to her were blurred. Maybe if Brian had found a pattern in his lists, I'd have had something to look forward to. But I didn't hear from him.

A few days before the protest, my English teacher handed

back my report on Shakespearean theaters. She gave me an *A* and praised me for doing such a good job. "I admire your keeping up with your work so well after what happened. If there is anything I can do to help . . ."

Because I'd promised Alice, I said, "My aunt is part of a relatives' group that is demonstrating at the airline office on Sunday for increased security. I know it's short notice, but if you could spread the word . . ."

That's all my English teacher had to hear. She volunteered to announce it at the teachers' meeting that afternoon. She said she'd speak to the art teacher about publicity posters. Before the week was over, there were posters all over the school, and ten different people—including Jill and Melinda—told me they would see me at the protest. I had no choice. I had to go to the protest.

⬤━⬤━⬤

On the day of the protest, the living room was stacked with boxes of signs and armbands, people were coming from a hundred miles around, and Channel 5 News had promised to cover the action. There was an excitement in the air that was even reaching me.

Alice was on the telephone arranging last-minute details and cutting black armbands at the same time. She snipped away with the phone tucked between her ear and shoulder. When the phone slipped and clattered to the floor, I offered, "I'll finish the armbands."

She handed me the construction paper and scissors. Covering the mouthpiece with her hand, she whispered, "I'm glad you changed your mind and decided to come along."

There was no point in telling her that I'd been forced to change my mind. I said, "There's the doorbell. Should I answer it?"

"That's Mr. Gordon. He and Brian are driving us to the protest."

After the boxes of signs and armbands were loaded into

the car, there was barely room for Mr. Gordon and Alice to squeeze in. Brian and I had to go by subway.

The subway is slow on Sunday. We waited forever for our train. Then it stalled on the Manhattan Bridge. By the time we got to the protest, it was in full swing. I couldn't believe the size of the crowd. Fifth Avenue was jammed with people wearing black armbands, chanting and shouting, and waving signs saying MAKE THE SKIES SAFE and NO MORE VICTIMS. It was really exciting.

Left to myself, I'd have hung back and watched for a while. Kind of gotten my feet wet gradually. Brian took to the noise and excitement like an Olympic diver plunging into a pool. He dragged me through the crowd to where Alice and his father were giving out signs and armbands. Brian got himself a black armband and handed me a sign with a picture of a bomb with a red slash through it.

Jill spotted me carrying my sign. She asked if there were any more signs. I gave her mine. She thought I'd painted it. I had to admit I hadn't. When Jill marched happily away waving the sign, I went back to Alice for an armband. I'm more comfortable wearing a small armband than carrying a big sign.

Before I could get my armband on, Alice said, "There are the TV guys." She grabbed my hand and headed for them.

There were two reporters. One had a camcorder on his shoulder, and the other was holding a microphone. Alice introduced herself. Then she pushed me forward. "This is my niece, Lisa Barnett. Her parents were on the plane."

The man with the camcorder turned it on me. I felt shy and embarrassed and excited and important, all at once. It was awesome to think that the whole country would see me on the news tonight. I wished I were wearing my armband. I didn't know whether to smile or look serious.

Alice knew exactly what to do when the camera turned on her. She looked straight into it and spoke in a clear, confident voice. "We are the relatives and friends of the people who died in the recent crash of the London to New York plane. We are here to ask for a full investigation into how a bomb was smuggled onto the plane. We are calling for stronger security for all flights at all airports. We also want laws spelling out what airlines must do in case of disaster to help the victims and their families. We are determined that other people will not suffer as we and our loved ones have suffered."

When Brian appeared at my side, I whispered, "Isn't Alice doing great? Who'd have thought she could be so dignified." I strained to catch every word. It was hard to hear because there was so much noise and confusion. Cars were honking in the street and people were milling around talking, chanting, and singing.

The noise seemed to be getting louder and louder. It took me a while to realize that most of the noise was coming from down the block. The reporters realized it, too. The guy with the microphone said, "I hear trouble." The cameraman answered, "Let's go."

Without any equipment to carry, Alice was faster than both of them. She plunged into the crowd and headed toward the sound of trouble.

Alice is a champion pusher. A path opened for her. I followed close behind her. Brian followed me. As we got nearer to the trouble, the crowd thickened. It became harder to move. Alice shoved through the press of bodies without bothering to see if I was keeping up.

People got between us. I fell farther and farther behind. I called to Alice to wait. Either she didn't hear or she pretended not to hear. Soon she was so far ahead that I could just see the back of her red sweatshirt between two blue uniforms. Then she disappeared.

I was struck by a sudden fear that something awful was going to happen to her. That I couldn't imagine what might happen only made my panic worse. I struggled to reach her.

Brian grabbed my shoulder. "You won't get through that way."

Ned pulled me back from the edge of the stage. "Be you all right?"

Dazed by the sudden shift, I gasped, "I think so."

"Then let us quit this place before some oaf cracks our pates."

Looking around, I saw what he meant. Fights had broken out all over the place. Fists were socking jaws and cudgels were hitting *pates* (heads) all around us. I couldn't see Rooji anywhere. Frightened for her, I insisted, "I have to find Rooji . . . I mean, Robin. Did you see him? He was wearing a red lady-in-waiting costume."

"If that were him in the red robe, he was getting a drubbing near the dressing room."

"We have to save him!"

Brian was holding onto my shoulder. I tore at his restraining hand. "Let me go!"

"Ow! You made me bleed." He sucked the scratch on his wrist.

Although I didn't see any blood, I apologized. "I'm sorry. I didn't mean to scratch you. But I have to save Alice."

"Save her from what?"

"I have this strange feeling that something awful is going to happen. I have to find her."

He shrugged. "If it's so desperate, try working your way around the edge of the crowd."

I wriggled toward the nearest open space, expecting him to follow me. He just stood examining the tiny scratch like it needed stitches. I asked, "Aren't you coming?"

"Say 'please.' "

There was no time to argue. I swallowed my pride. "Please."

"Say 'pretty please with sugar on it'."

No way! Then the crowd's noise rose another ten decibels. I mumbled, "Pretty please with sugar on it."

"That's better. Now I'll lead the way."

Ned pulled me toward the dressing room. "I see Robin's red robe. Methinks he is in trouble."

Brian said, "I see Alice's red sweatshirt. It looks like she's in trouble with the cops."

Rooji was struggling to hold off a brawny blacksmith's 'prentice. I yelled, "Hang on! We're coming!"

Brian demanded, "Why are you standing with your mouth open like you're hypnotized?" Then it dawned on him. "You went back. How?"

"I told you, I don't know." I grabbed his hand. "Come on. We have to save her." With all the switching back and forth I wasn't sure who I meant.

Brian didn't move. "That's it! I've been going over and over the lists we made and not getting anywhere. It just hit me."

I couldn't believe he was talking about his stupid lists while who knew what kind of awful thing was happening. I hissed through gritted teeth, "If you don't help me now, I'll never forgive you as long as I live."

"Don't get yourself in a stew. Okay, we'll find your aunt now and talk about it later."

But by the time we got through to where Brian had seen Alice with the cops, she was gone.

chapter
13

Alice was in jail. Jill had been right on the spot, and she'd seen the whole thing. When Jill spotted me searching for Alice, she couldn't wait to tell me what happened. She said that the trouble began because the protesters were blocking traffic. Although they were supposed to stay on the sidewalk, there were so many people that they overflowed into the street. Cars couldn't get through. Drivers honked and yelled.

Jill described the cops setting up blue wooden barriers along the curb: POLICE LINE—DO NOT CROSS. When one protester refused to move out of the way, an officer dropped a barrier in front of him and used it to prod him onto the sidewalk. The protester complained angrily about being herded like cattle, but he backed up—right into a white-haired old lady. She lost her balance and fell. Someone yelled that the cops had knocked down a frail, innocent old lady.

There were shouts of "Police brutality." The crowd surged toward the barriers. The police took up their crowd-control positions. The people up front tried to get out of the way while the people in back pushed forward. In the confusion, two college guys were shoved into the line of cops. The cops, thinking they were being attacked, arrested them. The guys insisted that they hadn't done anything. The cops refused to listen.

Jill said that Alice arrived on the scene as the cops bundled the college guys into a police car. Alice demanded,

"Release those boys immediately! I organized this protest. If you are determined to arrest someone, arrest me."

An officer informed Alice that she hadn't done anything to be arrested for. She thought that over. Then she took a sign from another protester. The sign said FIGHT FOR SAFETY. Alice hit the cop with it.

I didn't want to believe it. I wanted Alice to be the person who gave that inspiring interview to the TV reporters. I wanted her to be an aunt I could live with and be proud of. But the sick feeling in my stomach told me the story was true. It was exactly what you'd expect from Alice. What I should have expected.

Brian said, "Wow! Alice is really cool." Which is just what you'd expect from him.

I dragged Brian away before he could give Jill any more gossip to spread all over school tomorrow. I said we had to go find Brian's father right away and tell him what happened.

Mr. Gordon didn't think Alice was so cool. Out of consideration for my feelings, he didn't say that she had to be crazy to hit a cop. Instead he said that it was unfortunate when an individual let emotion interfere with what the group was trying to accomplish. I got the message and squirmed with embarrassment. I tried to refuse his offer to drive me home when the protest was over, but he insisted.

He dropped me in front of Alice's house. He promised, "I'll call my lawyer and ask him to try to arrange your aunt's release. However, I'm afraid it may take a while."

I thanked him for his help and ran up the steps, anxious to get away from his unspoken disapproval. I knew he had me lumped with Alice in his mind: like aunt, like niece. There was no sense protesting I'd sooner be a filthy panhandler annoying people on the street than be like Alice. He'd just think I was disloyal. I unlocked the door and ducked inside.

Luckily, I had my key with me. Or was it luck? Alice, who is usually careless about such things, had reminded me twice to take my key in case we got separated. Had she planned to get arrested? Had she done it deliberately for the publicity? How could she do that to me? I felt hurt and betrayed.

I nursed my hurt feelings while I made myself a goat cheese sandwich on black bread (that's all there was) and opened a can of cat food for Bathsheba. Then I sat down in front of the TV with my sandwich. I switched on the evening news. Maybe it wasn't as bad as Jill said. Maybe she'd exaggerated.

I sat through a crisis in Russia, a military takeover in the Caribbean, a filibuster in the Senate, and a scandal in Hollywood. Then, when I had almost stopped expecting it, there was the protest in full living color.

I needn't have worried about whether to smile for the reporters. They never showed me. Nor did they show Alice's lovely interview. What filled the screen was Alice bopping a cop over the head with a FIGHT FOR SAFETY sign. She looked like she was having the time of her life.

I punched the OFF button. Because the remote was different from ours at home, I hit VOLUME by accident. Alice's kung fu yell echoed through the room. I shuddered. Was that what my English teacher had put the notice on the bulletin board for? Had the other girls from school come to the protest to see that? How would I face them tomorrow?

I pushed the right button, and the screen went blank. I tried to read a book while I ate my sandwich. I couldn't concentrate or swallow. I threw the sandwich in the garbage and went down to the office to see to Rex. Alice hadn't worried about what would happen to him while she was in jail. Any more than she had worried about me.

Rex looked up as I opened his cage. I petted him and gave him fresh food and water. He whimpered when I closed the cage door. I said, "You don't want to stay in there all by yourself, do you? I'll take you up to my room. If Alice doesn't like it, that's too bad. She shouldn't have abandoned you."

The back stairs are steep. I was afraid Rex wasn't strong

enough to climb them. I picked him up and carried him. Although he was heavier than I expected, I didn't mind. He felt snug and warm against me.

I put him down on the Hide-A-Bed and closed the door so Bathsheba wouldn't wander in. He looked around and sniffed. Then, satisfied that this was a good place, he put his head down between his paws.

"Hey, don't go to sleep. Keep me company."

He looked up inquiringly.

"Mr. Gordon's lawyer should be getting Alice out soon. Do you think the cops fingerprinted her? Or handcuffed her? It might teach her a lesson. Mom always told me I had to learn from the consequences of my actions. Maybe a few hours in jail will teach Alice responsibility."

Rex growled. He couldn't understand everything I said, but I thought he sensed how I felt.

"As soon as Alice does something right, she has to turn around and wreck it. Like she's going out of her way to prove that my parents made an awful mistake to appoint her my guardian." I stroked Rex's head. "If Mom had her way I'd be living with a normal family now instead of worrying what weird thing Alice will do next. When Mom and Dad decided that Grandma was too old to take care of me if anything happened to them, Mom wanted my guardian to be her friend in Chicago who has two kids. I know she did. I heard her discussing it with Dad. What could have made her change her mind? Maybe she figured it didn't matter because nothing was going to happen to them. But it did happen. Why? Why of all the planes in the sky. . ."

The conversation was drifting in a direction I didn't intend. I jumped up. "Look at how long my fingernails are! No wonder I scratched Brian. I'd better cut them before he has an excuse to make another fuss."

Rex fell asleep while I was giving myself a manicure. Although it was lonely without him to talk to, I knew he was weak and needed his sleep. So I cleaned out my book bag and reorganized my loose-leaf. Then I went searching for an iron to press a blouse for school tomorrow. To my surprise, I found both an iron and an ironing board in a closet. Not to my surprise, the iron was caked with burned-on gunk. I did a thorough job of cleaning it. Then I took out all my clothes that had gotten wrinkled when we brought them over from the old apartment.

As I ironed, I kept thinking I heard footsteps on the stoop. At each sound, I went into the pose of someone so busy with what she's doing that she doesn't hear the front door open. But the door never opened.

When I ran out of wrinkled clothes, I took a shower and washed my hair. Time dragged like I was pushing it uphill. Finally, I went to bed. I curled up with my feet against Rex and tried to sleep.

I might as well have tried to fly. I kept hearing noises in the dark. When I held my breath to listen, the noise stopped. When I breathed normally, my breath seemed to cover the sound of sneaky footsteps. I told myself that old houses make strange noises. I told myself to think about something else.

I thought about Rooji. It had been wonderful running away to London with her, being in a theater company with her, and helping her get an acting role. Why couldn't it stay wonderful? It wasn't fair for Rooji's dreams to fall apart. It wasn't fair for her to be fighting to defend herself against a bully twice her size. How long could she hold out? My best friend, my other self, was in terrible danger, and I was three thousand miles and four hundred years away. All I could do was wait for a sudden switch back to her.

Unless Brian's idea—whatever it was—worked. I wanted to believe that he was onto something, but he might just be showing off. Or maybe he was kidding himself. I sensed that he had some hidden reason for searching for the key to the past. All those questions he asked made me uncomfortable. Not the questions about what I was doing before and after the switches. Questions about my knowing what happened in the past when I wasn't there, and didn't Rooji miss me. And, of course, the time differences.

I would never have thought about the time difference if Brian hadn't put it into my head. Now it bothered me. I'd left Rooji in the middle of the riot. Although almost two weeks had gone by in the present, the riot was still going strong when I got back to her. I'd told Brian that there was no rule that time had to move at the same rate in the past and the present. But how did I get back to the exact moment when Rooji was in the worst trouble? Did she call out to me when she needed me? Or did I go to her when I needed her?

It was ridiculous to lie in the dark worrying about Brian's dumb questions. I sat up and switched on the lamp. I picked up my math book and forced myself to review distance problems. "If two trains are traveling away from each other and one is moving three times as fast . . ."

Eventually the math made me sleepy. I turned out the light and dozed off.

Rex's growling woke me. I sat up and clutched the covers to my chest. It wasn't my imagination this time. Those were real footsteps. They were coming toward my room!

My door inched open. I put my hand on Rex's head. A figure stepped into the room. I yelled, "Sic 'em!"

Rex ran toward the figure, sniffed her, and sat down at her feet. Alice asked, "What's going on? You scared me half to death."

"I scared you! You sneaked into my room like a robber."

"I was checking that you got home safely."

She had taken her own sweet time getting around to thinking about me. The lighted numbers of the digital electric clock I'd brought from home said 2:02 A.M. I asked, "How was jail?"

Alice pretended not to hear the sarcasm in my voice. (Or was she so thick-skinned that she really didn't hear it?) "Not quite as awful as I expected. Although the red tape was unbelievable. I had to fill out more forms than when I applied to veterinary school. When they finally let me make a phone call, I called my friend Erica who is a lawyer. Mr. Gordon's lawyer showed up before she did and arranged bail. When Erica arrived, she insisted that I was a responsible citizen and should be released on my own recognizance. Erica was upset at having to undo everything Mr. Gordon's lawyer had done, and he was angry about coming out on a Sunday for nothing. Things got so tense that I was tempted to stay in jail."

"Why didn't you?"

"It wasn't a very pleasant place. Besides, I have to operate in the morning."

"I should've guessed you'd worry about your work."

She gave me a long, thoughtful look. "Why are you angry at me?"

"Why should I be angry?"

Alice cleared her throat. "I followed my conscience. If you think what I did was wrong, tell me why."

"If you don't know, I can't explain it to you." I lay down with my back to her, pulled up the covers, and waited for her to leave.

She didn't leave. She yanked the covers away, grabbed me under my arms, hauled me into a sitting position, and shouted, "Speak to me! You're as bad as your mother with that silent treatment."

Although I didn't enjoy being yanked around like a puppet, there was a certain satisfaction in seeing how childish and irresponsible she was. How could I be expected to talk to such a person? And how dare she criticize my mother! My mother never lost her temper or laid a hand on me or hit a cop. My mother never made me ashamed of her. The only thing Mom ever did wrong in her whole life was to leave me with Alice.

Suddenly I needed my mother so badly that a wave of pain welled up from deep inside my chest and threatened to drown me. When I tried to breathe, I could only make a queer gurgling sound.

Alice let go of me. "Are you all right?"

I shook my head violently. The head shake was saying "No" to everything: to the plane crash, to Alice not being like Mom, to Mom and Dad being dead.

She misunderstood. "I didn't mean to hurt you. I've had a hard night, and my temper ran away with me. I'm sorry."

What good was her being sorry when she was sorry for the wrong things? When I was drowning? I struggled for air. There was no air. The gurgling sound got louder.

I seemed to be looking at Alice through binoculars from the wrong side. I saw her take aim from far away. It took a long time for her hand to reach my cheek. I had time to think: you're only supposed to slap a person who is hysterical, and I'm not hysterical.

The shock and pain of the slap made me gasp. Air rushed into my lungs—and burst out again in a loud wail. I started to cry. Once I started, I couldn't stop. I cried fiercely and desperately.

Alice patted my back gently. I pulled away from her hand, rejecting any comfort she could offer, clinging to my pain and desperation. I cried and cried. I cried until my eyes were swollen almost shut and my nose was totally clogged.

When I was finally cried out, I mopped my eyes and blew my nose, carefully keeping my back to Alice. I was ashamed of my outburst and afraid of her reaction. Muttering that I needed to wash my face, I ran to the bathroom. I hid in the bathroom as long as I dared. When I slunk back into my room, she was sitting on my bed examining Rex.

I'd steeled myself against Alice being mad at my treating her like poison ivy when she tried to comfort me. I was prepared to resist her pressuring me to tell her why I was crying. I wouldn't even have been surprised if she said it was all her fault for roughing me up. What I could never have dreamt of in a million years was her totally ignoring what happened. She said, "Rex is recovering nicely. Would you like him for a pet?"

I stammered, "What about his owners? He's a pure-blooded beagle. He must be worth a lot of money."

"His current owners only took him as a favor. If I don't charge for his care, they'll probably feel that they came out ahead."

"What about Bathsheba? Cats and dogs don't get along."

"They do if they're handled right. Look, Lisa, it was only an idea. If you don't want Rex, say so."

"I do want him!" I couldn't bear the thought of losing him.

"Then why argue with me? I swear, I don't understand you."

"Well, I don't understand you either."

Alice said, "I guess we'll have to settle for that for tonight. I'll get a dog bed from the office. Rex shouldn't get into the habit of sleeping with you."

"Can't he just stay tonight? Please." I'd never have tried to wheedle Mom like that. It wouldn't have worked.

For once, I was glad Alice wasn't like Mom. She gave in. "I guess one night won't hurt. There isn't much left of it anyway. Now we'd better get some sleep. I have to operate early tomorrow, and you have school."

chapter 14

Rex nuzzled his nose into my neck. Sleepily, I stroked his smooth fur. Having him share my bed made me feel warm and safe. He licked my face. I pressed deeper into my pillow. His rough tongue followed me.

"Stop that." I opened my eyes reluctantly—and caught sight of the clock. It was nearly eight! I'd forgotten to set my alarm last night, and Alice never thought to check if I was up this morning. I'd have slept until noon if Rex hadn't wakened me.

By rushing like mad, I got to school a second before the late bell rang. My homeroom teacher was taking attendance as I tiptoed in. She called, "Lisa Barnett." When I said "Here," the whole class turned to stare as if nobody had ever been late for homeroom before. Then I saw Jill whispering to Melinda, and I knew why they were all looking at me. I wanted to dig a hole in the floor and crawl into it.

The bell rang for first period. I pretended to be looking for something in my book bag. I kept up the imaginary search until everyone had left the room. Then I made a dash for my class.

By using the bag-search tactic, I managed to avoid talking to anyone all morning. My luck ran out before lunch. Jill came up behind me as I pawed through my book bag. "What did you lose?"

I stuttered, "My . . . my pen." I can never lie without sounding like I have a speech impediment.

"Look later. Melinda is saving us seats in the cafeteria."
Jill took my arm so I couldn't make a run for it. I felt like a
prisoner being led to the gas chamber. Except I couldn't hope
for it to be over quickly.

Melinda and practically every other girl I knew were
sitting at a long table with two empty chairs at the head. Jill
took one chair and pushed me into the other. As if they'd
been waiting to start a meeting, everyone began talking
about the protest. The girls who had been there described it
to those who'd missed it. The girls who'd seen it on TV put
in their two cents. Even those who wouldn't recognize a
protest if they tripped over one at high noon had something
to say. I wished I could disappear in a puff of smoke.

They were all talking at once, so I couldn't hear exactly
what each person said. But I could imagine. To hide my
embarrassment and shame, I made a production of unwrap-
ping my sandwich—stale black bread with some eggplant
glop I'd found lurking in back of the refrigerator. Maybe if I
seemed so hungry that all I could think of was food the girls
would talk around me the way they usually did. Maybe
they'd forget I was there.

As I bit into the sandwich, Jill's voice rose above the
babble. "You can't really know what it was like unless you
were carrying a protest sign in the thick of things. There
was a wonderful feeling of being part of something exciting
and important. And Lisa's aunt was so brave. I was right
there when she stood up to the cops and went to jail to
protect those college guys. It was awesome."

I couldn't believe that Jill was talking like Alice was some
kind of hero. I sneaked glances at the other girls as Jill gave
them a blow-by-blow description of Alice versus the cops.
They looked impressed and admiring. Were they crazy or
was I?

Jill finished her story and decided to share the spotlight.
She asked, "Lisa, is your aunt still in jail?"

Everyone waited for my answer. I took another bite of my

sandwich and muttered through the dry mouthful, "Her lawyer got her out late last night."

Then the questions came at me thick and fast. "What was jail like?" "Did they lock Alice up in a cell?" "How long did they keep her?" "How much was her bail?" "Was she scared?" Reluctantly, I repeated what Alice had told me about the red tape, the bail problem, and the conflict between Erica and Mr. Gordon's lawyer. The girls lapped it up.

Melinda said, "What an ordeal for your aunt." She didn't seem to understand that Alice had brought it on herself. Did she expect the cop to stand there smiling while Alice bopped him over the head?

Jill asked, "When will the trial be?"

Until Jill asked, it hadn't occurred to me that Alice could be dragged into court like some sleazy shoplifter. I said, "Alice didn't mention a trial, so I guess there won't be one."

Melinda, whose older sister goes to law school, insisted, "There has to be a trial. A short one if your aunt pleads guilty. That way she'll probably get off with a fine. If she decides to fight, the trial could last for weeks and who knows what could happen."

Jill said, "A long trial would be good publicity for the cause. Alice could make a speech about why she was protesting. Maybe she'll be on TV again."

My stomach churned at the mere thought of it. That awful eggplant glop threatened to come up. "Excuse me. I have to go to the bathroom." I tried not to run.

⊸⊷⊶

When I finally got back to Brooklyn after school, I found Brian waiting on the stoop. As soon as he saw me, he started in. "I kept trying to find a pattern in the lists we made. When I said you looked hypnotized at the protest, it hit me."

As the saying goes: Hope springs eternal. I asked, "What hit you?"

"You used the word 'hypnotic' about the picture over the sofa, and you tried to hypnotize yourself. It made me remember seeing a TV program about a woman who went back to her previous lives under hypnosis."

"So?"

"So I called one of my brother's friends who knows about these things. I let him think I wanted to learn hypnosis for a party stunt. He said he could teach me to hypnotize you in a few hours."

I should have known better than to hope Brian would come up with something that made sense. "Forget it. I'm not letting you mess around with my mind. Now don't start nagging because I won't listen."

Telling him not to nag was like telling him not to breathe. He began, "I'm not just doing this for you. I have my own reasons for learning how to get back to the past. And you owe me."

I'd had a hard day and I was in no mood. "I don't owe you anything. I paid you back for the soda. Everything else you did was your own idea. So leave me alone." I started up the stairs.

He blocked my way. "I know that hypnosis will work. Once I learn how to send you back into the past, I'll teach you to do it for me. I'll go back and warn my brother not to take the plane."

If I'd been up to sparing any real thought for Brian, I'd have realized that he'd never given up on warning his brother. That was why he'd knocked himself out with the library and the lists and learning hypnosis. I couldn't help feeling sorry for him because I knew it was impossible. I said, "Even supposing the hypnosis works, what makes you think that of all the times and places in the past you'll end up at the London airport just in time to tell your brother to take another plane?"

"You always go back to Rooji because that's where you want to be. I'll go back to my brother because that's where I want to be."

Although he made it sound reasonable, I knew that what Brian wanted to do was completely different from what I was doing with Rooji. I tried to think of a way to explain the difference to him.

Brian took advantage of my hesitation. "Please listen. I never told this to anyone before. I was jealous of my brother. Because he was older than me, he did everything first. When he stood on his head or earned a Boy Scout badge, my mother thought he was wonderful. When I did the same things later on, she just said, 'Very nice, Brian.' Even now, all she does is cry for him like I'm not there. That's why I have to go back and find him."

I tried to ease his guilt. "I'm sure you weren't just jealous of your brother. I'm sure you loved him, too."

"I did. That's why I have to see him again. Even if I can't save him, I can at least tell him I'm sorry. Won't you help me?"

How could I refuse?

chapter
15

The following Saturday, I leaned back in the living-room easy chair with Rex at my feet. I didn't like handing over control of my mind to Brian or anyone else, but I'd promised to let him hypnotize me. Besides, it was nearly a week since I'd left Rooji at the mercy of the 'prentice with the cudgel. I hadn't been able to get back to her on my own.

Brian took a gold pendant on a chain out of his pocket. I tried to relax while he swung the pendant slowly back and forth. He repeated in a monotonous voice, "You are getting tired. Very tired. You are getting sleepy. Very sleepy."

I started to get slightly sleepy. Then Rex growled. I reached down to quiet him.

———

Ned and I fought our way through the mob toward Rooji's red robe. Before we could reach her, the tough 'prentice knocked her down. I watched in helpless horror as he raised his cudgel to hit her again.

Then, like a brown streak of lightning, a dog leapt from nowhere and fastened his jaws on the bully's arm. The 'prentice yelped and dropped the cudgel. Rex held on while Ned and I dragged Rooji to safety. When Rex finally let go, the 'prentice turned and ran. Rex came after us barking happily.

———

"Quiet, Rex," Brian commanded. "I can't hypnotize Lisa with you barking."

I said, "You already did."

When I explained what had happened, Brian asked, "Are you telling me that Rex went into the past with you because you were touching him when you went under?"

I nodded. "He saved Rooji. Do you have a doggie treat I can give him?" Although Alice had warned me not to over-feed Rex, he deserved a reward.

Brian took a treat out of his pocket. Rex gulped it down.

Then Brian fished in his pocket again. He pulled out some of the red string they tie around bakery boxes. (What other junk did he have in there?) "If Rex can do it, so can I. I need my right hand for the pendant, so I'll tie our left wrists together. That way I'll go along with you next time."

Puzzled, I asked, "Why? I thought the idea was for me to learn to hypnotize you if it worked on me."

"If it worked."

"I just told you it worked. Don't you believe me?"

"People believe what they want to believe."

I demanded, "What is that supposed to mean?"

"It could mean that I want to believe in going back to the past, or that you want to believe in Rooji. Or it could just mean that I want to see for myself."

"Or it could mean that you're pulling one of your obnoxious stunts." It had to be a stunt. Brian had believed me from the minute I first told him about Rooji. Why should he start doubting now?

The insult rolled right off him. He asked, "Are you afraid to let me try it?"

"I'm not afraid. I just resent your saying . . ."

We were still arguing when Alice came up from the office where she'd been doing the accounts on the computer.

I said, "Alice, you remember Brian Gordon, don't you?"

She said, "Oh. I meant to thank Brian's father for driving you home after the protest." Like she usually got around to things like that and this just slipped her mind.

Brian said, "No problem. I'll tell him." I didn't know he could act so polite.

Alice acted polite, too. She said, "Thank you." Then she nodded toward the pendant lying on the sofa. "That's pretty. Whose is it?"

I said, "It's Brian's." He looked embarrassed and stuffed the pendant back into his pocket. I let him suffer a little before I explained, "Brian learned to do hypnosis. He was trying it on me."

Alice said, "I don't think that's such a good idea. Hypnosis is not a game. It can have serious consequences if it's misused." She sounded just like a mother. Maybe she was learning.

Anyway, it got me off the hook. I said, "We won't anymore." Brian gave me a you-coward look. I answered with a my-aunt-won't-let-me look.

Brian turned to Alice. "I thought what you did at the protest was cool. It came over great on TV."

She looked pleased. "Too bad they didn't show my interview instead. But any kind of publicity helps. My lawyer thinks we might get news coverage of my trial if she can get it scheduled soon."

"Trial!" It just burst out of me. "You didn't say anything about a trial to me." Alice had let me convince myself that the girls at school were wrong about a trial, that there wouldn't be one.

She answered mildly, "I didn't mention it because I wasn't sure I had a good case. Erica needed time to research it. She called while I was down in the office to give me the okay."

"Why do you have to go to trial? On cop shows on TV, criminals are always plea-bargaining and getting off with light sentences. Especially if they didn't mean what they did.

Can't you just say you're sorry and pay a fine or something?"
Even as I pleaded, I knew it was hopeless.

"Maybe if I were a criminal I'd plea-bargain. But I'm not.
Neither do I feel that I did anything wrong. I was protecting
the college kids—and exercising my rights to free speech
and assembly. Erica says she can present a good defense
based on either one of those points."

Erica would enjoy presenting a good defense. Alice would
have a ball being the center of attention and making
speeches. Brian would think it was all cool. And I would die
of shame.

Then an even more horrible thought hit me. "What if the
verdict is *Guilty*? Couldn't you go to jail?"

"Erica says that's not likely."

"But it's possible, isn't it?"

"Yes, it's possible. That is a chance I have to take."

Of all the irresponsible things Alice had pulled, this was
the absolute worst. As long as she had her day in court, she
didn't care what happened to Rex and me if she ended up in
the Women's House of Detention. If Alice was so anxious to
go to jail, let her. I hoped they locked her up and threw away
the key.

◖—◗

Rooji said, "I cannot forgive Master Bowen. It is his fault
that the theater is being closed."

I asked, "Why is it Master Bowen's fault?"

"He and the actor who plays the king were in it together.
Because they thought the queen's new taxes unfair, they
added to the witch speech after the lord chamberlain's office
approved the play."

I blamed the duke's agent for tattling to the lord chamberlain. And the duke for not protecting us. A word from the
duke in the right ear and I'd be watching Rooji act right
now. But I didn't want to argue with her when she looked so
pale. The purple lump on her forehead from the cudgel blow

stood out against her white face. I said soothingly, "Master Greene said the theater would reopen as soon as Master Bowen apologizes and his apology is accepted."

"If he apologizes. If it is accepted. Where will we stay in the meanwhile? With the theater closed, we cannot sleep on our pallets in the dressing room as we usually do."

"Master Greene will probably send us to stay with the actors who live at the inn."

Rooji wailed, "We would have to share their beds, and they would discover that we are girls."

I hadn't thought of that. "Couldn't we go to your cousin Will?" Imagine actually meeting William Shakespeare.

She shook her head fiercely. It made her dizzy, and her face turned even paler. "Cousin Will would send me home to Stratford. I would never get a chance to act. I cannot go home. I must act! I must!"

She sounded frantic. As strongly as she felt about acting, it wasn't like her to carry on this way. Maybe Ned was right about a blow on the head addling a person's wits. I put my arm around her. "Relax. We'll think of something."

Suddenly she gagged, ran to the slop bucket, and threw up. Now I was really worried about her. I had to get her to a doctor for X rays. But the nearest X-ray machine was four hundred years in the future.

‑●‑●‑●‑

Brian was telling Alice he'd noticed the X-ray machine and operating room downstairs. He asked her what kind of operations she performed. As she described them, I realized how much a vet was like a doctor. Alice would know what to do for Rooji.

I interrupted, "How would a doctor treat a person who got hit on the head and then didn't seem like herself and was pale and threw up?"

Although Alice seemed surprised at the question, she answered, "It sounds like a simple concussion. However, the doctor might want to rule out a hemorrhage or skull fracture with a CAT scan or an MRI."

"What if there were no CAT scans or MRIs? What if it was long ago, like in Shakespeare's time?"

"Is this for your English class? Well, in the sixteenth century doctors were more likely to kill patients than to cure them. Doctors believed in bleeding patients—opening their veins and letting out lots of blood. The knives they used were filthy. Infections and blood poisoning were common. Someone with a concussion in those days would be much better off staying away from doctors and resting in bed for a few days."

I knew what I had to do. I couldn't stop Alice from having her trial, but I could stop some quack from killing Rooji. At least, I hoped I could.

I waited until Alice went into the kitchen for a snack— although what she'd find, I couldn't imagine. Then I told Brian, "I'm going to take Rex for a walk in the park. Why don't you come along?"

I was getting to know the park. I led the way down a tree-lined side path. When we reached a quiet spot, I told Brian, "What Alice said about old-time doctors scared me."

I hadn't expected him to make it easy for me. He didn't. He said, "Did you know that doctors bled George Washington to death when all he had was a sore throat?"

"All the more reason for me to see that it doesn't happen to Rooji."

"I wish you luck."

I knew I'd have to grovel. I tried to get it over with fast. "Okay. I'm asking you to hypnotize me. I'll let you tie our wrists together if you want."

He drew it out. "Didn't I hear you tell Alice we weren't going to fool around with hypnosis anymore?"

"This is an emergency. Besides, Alice is a fine one to talk about what people should and shouldn't do. If she were me, do you think she'd let anything stop her?"

Finally, Brian tied our wrists and got out his pendant. I leaned against a tree and stared up at the leaves moving in the breeze.

●◗●

A leaf fell. I was in the yard of Ned's father's shop. Ned said, "Surely the physician you saw should have bled Robin."

"He said bed rest was the newest cure from . . ." Then I remembered that anything Italian was considered special. "From Italy."

"The physician studied in Padua? He must have cost a pretty penny."

"He did, so we have to do exactly what he told me. Robin must rest in bed for three days. He must have a bed to himself and wear a night robe." When Ned still looked doubtful, I searched my mind for something to convince him. My eyes fell on the broken red string around my wrist. I said without stuttering, "We must put this red cord around Robin's wrist to draw out the evil humors."

●◗●

Brian stared at the red string dangling from our wrists. He accused me, "You broke it. You yanked your hand away and the string snapped."

"I didn't. It must've broken when I went back to Rooji. It's not my fault you didn't go along with me."

He didn't argue. He just played with his piece of the string. He pulled it, snapped it, and rolled it into a little ball, looking thoughtful. I couldn't tell what he was thinking.

I said, "Ned believed that the string was a special cure. It convinced him to put Rooji's pallet in a shed in the yard. She can rest out the concussion there."

Brian just kept fooling with the string. Then, like he'd suddenly made up his mind, he said, "We'll give it one more try. But we need something stronger. I have a set of hand-cuffs at home."

Although I didn't like the idea, I couldn't think of a good reason to refuse. "Alice has a meeting of her veterinary society next Saturday. I saw it on the kitchen calendar. We could try then."

chapter
16

The next Saturday, I sat in the lumpy armchair in my room. I'd closed the door in case Alice came back from her meeting early. She hadn't bothered to tell me when to expect her. I wriggled around in the chair trying to get comfortable while Brian swung his pendant and told me I was getting sleepy. I didn't get either comfortable or sleepy.

Brian accused, "You're not cooperating."

"I'm cooperating as much as I can while I'm drowning in sweat. It must be a hundred and twenty degrees in this stupid room. How can we have such heat at the end of May?"

"It's the beginning of June."

"Alice promised me an air conditioner. I'll be lucky to see it by the end of August."

He ignored my complaints. "You are getting tired. Very tired."

I was getting tired of the whole thing. Brian had been trying to hypnotize me for an hour. I couldn't help being glad it wasn't working. I didn't really want him going back to the past with me. It was my world. I didn't want him tramping around there asking questions. As long as Ned was taking good care of Rooji . . .

"Pay attention!"

"I can't. These handcuffs are rubbing a hole in my wrist. Let's take a break."

When he took the handcuffs off, I rubbed my wrist and checked the date on my watch calendar. "It really is June. I can't believe that the term is almost over. It's like it went by while I wasn't looking. Yet, when I think about it, the time seems to have dragged on forever. You know what I mean?"

He wasn't listening. He started snapping the handcuffs open and shut, open and shut. It was really annoying.

I said, "Stop that. I can take a hint. I'll try again." I held my wrist out for the cuff.

"No."

"You mean you don't want to try anymore? I thought you were set on going back with me and seeing for yourself."

"I've seen enough. I see what's really going on."

I didn't like his tone. "What do you mean by that?"

"You should know what I mean. Think about it."

"I don't know, and I don't want to think about it. I've spent all afternoon in this oven staring at that stupid pendant because you asked me to. If you don't appreciate it, go home and leave me alone."

Any reasonable person would have said he was sorry. Brian stamped out as if I was in the wrong.

●—●—●

I kept expecting Brian to show up on Alice's stoop. He didn't. I told myself I was glad not to have him annoying me while I was studying for finals. But I still hadn't heard from him when school ended. Neither had I made a switch back to Rooji.

I'd always looked forward to summer vacation because my parents always made interesting plans for me. When I was younger, I went to camp. When I became old enough to appreciate it, I traveled with Mom and Dad. Dad had suggested the Grand Canyon for this summer. Mom had talked about Hawaii. It never occurred to Alice to wonder what I was going to do with myself all summer. She said something about Manhattan Beach (which was really in Brooklyn) and art courses at the Brooklyn Museum, and let it go at that.

During the term, while I'd been in school for most of the day, Alice and I had drifted into the habit of keeping out of each other's way. When we found ourselves together, we talked about my schoolwork, the strange things that pet owners did, and what was on TV. Alice loved cop shows (figure that out) and hated hospital shows. I liked mysteries. We both enjoyed *Nature* and *National Geographic* specials. By keeping off the subjects we disagreed about—like the protest and Alice's upcoming trial—we managed to get along okay. The trouble started when school ended.

July arrived in a blast of heat and humidity. I still hadn't gotten an air conditioner for my room. Alice said she would move one from our old apartment. Then she decided that it added to the apartment's value. The apartment was a co-op, and she'd put it up for sale. She said the money would go into my college fund—like that made it right. Selling the apartment was one of the subjects I didn't discuss.

When she finally got around to buying me a new air conditioner, the store had to order the size I needed. Meanwhile I sweltered.

I tried to concentrate on *Little Women*. It was Mom's favorite book when she was my age. But it was too hot to read. Rex lay limp on the scruffy rug with his tongue lolling out. I knew just how he felt.

I was hot and lonely. In *Little Women*, the sisters had Marmee and one another. I didn't have anyone. I missed Rooji. I missed the girls' lunch talk at school. I even missed Brian.

I needed to talk to someone. I decided to call Jill, although I didn't know what to say without schoolwork to discuss. Her mother answered the phone. She said that Jill was visiting her married sister in Colorado for a few weeks. I said it wasn't important and Jill didn't have to bother calling me back. Then I flipped through my address book.

Brian's answering machine said that the family was at their summer home. I hoped that meant his mother was better, but it didn't help me. Everyone was doing something but me.

Another flip brought me to Grandma. I hadn't spoken to her lately. After she went back to Phoenix, she'd called every weekend. But she cried so much that I always hung up as soon as I could.

I went down to the office to ask Alice, "Can I call Grandma?"

She was busy with the billing. She nodded without taking her eyes off the computer screen.

I persisted, "Even though it isn't the weekend? Grandma always calls on weekends because long-distance rates are cheaper then."

Alice glanced at her watch. "Evening rates start at five. Why don't you wait a half hour?"

I waited until a quarter to five. Then I couldn't wait any longer. I dialed Grandma's number. After I assured her three times that nothing was wrong, Grandma was thrilled to hear from me. She said, "You sound so grown-up. Like your mother, may she rest in peace." I could hear the tears starting.

Quickly, I asked, "Did you know Mom when she was my age?"

"No. She met your father when she started teaching. He had been teaching for five years, and he was already the best teacher in the school. So when your mother had trouble with her class . . ."

I'd heard that story from Mom and Dad. (Actually I'd heard two different versions of it.) But I hadn't heard about how, when I was born, Mom and Dad decided to use their skills as teachers to give me the perfect upbringing, or how they stopped me from sucking my thumb, kept me from being afraid of the dentist, and introduced me to reading.

When Alice came up from the office, I repeated Grandma's stories to her word for word. She said "Really?" and "That's nice." But I could tell her mind was somewhere else.

The heat wave continued. It was too hot to go outside even if I'd had something to do or someone to do it with. My air conditioner finally came, so I stayed in my room until the walls started to close in on me. Then I wandered aimlessly around the house.

Every time I bumped into Alice, she got on my nerves more. She couldn't seem to do anything right. The house was a mess, the washing machine was broken, the dirty laundry collected in the closets and smelled in the heat, and the food—what there was of it—was impossible to stomach. In desperation, I starting pointing out where she was going wrong. I told her, "Mom always used to . . ." and "Dad always said . . ."

The first few times, Alice just shrugged. Then she started clearing her throat and saying things like, "To each her own," and "I guess you'll have to get used to my ways."

I couldn't bear her ways. It became like a contest: me pushing her to act properly, she stubbornly refusing, and both of us pretending it didn't matter. I got more and more frustrated, and Alice kept clearing her throat until the sound made me want to climb the walls. I wondered how long it would be before she exploded.

She lasted longer than I expected. Then one day it turned a bit cooler, and I ventured out to the library. I came back just as Alice was helping an old lady and her decrepit calico cat into a taxi. The old lady fussed over the cat, who seemed bored with the attention. When the taxi pulled away, Alice said with a smile, "That must be the most loved cat in town. She dines on braised calf's liver and sleeps on a silk cushion."

"Mom used to say there's something wrong with a world where rich people's pets get better care than poor people's children."

Alice didn't bother clearing her throat. She said in a voice tight with anger, "Perhaps your mother was an authority on education, culture, and keeping house. However, caring for animals is my work and I consider it worth doing. That old woman is far from rich, and that cat is the only thing she has to love in this world."

I don't know what possessed me to quote Mom as saying that about kids and animals. It just seemed the way she'd feel. But whatever else about Alice drove me crazy, I admired her dedication to her work. If she'd given me half a chance, I'd have said I was sorry.

She didn't give me a chance. She just turned and marched back into the house as if she couldn't bear the sight of me another second.

I waited for the whole silly thing to blow over. I waited for days for her to ask me if I'd like to see the monkey someone brought in for treatment or to suggest trying the new vegetarian restaurant on Union Street. I made up my mind to be enthusiastic about whatever she came up with. But she didn't suggest anything. She didn't stop talking to me or anything like that. She just acted as if she knew we could never be friends and she didn't care.

I couldn't believe that a thirty-one-year-old adult would nurse a grudge like a thirteen-year-old kid whose feelings are hurt. The longer Alice kept it up, the more disgusted I got. Two could play that game. I made a point of not being in the same room with her if I could possibly help it. If she came into the living room while I was watching TV, I went into my room to read even if it meant missing the end of a mystery. When I had to speak to her, I was barely polite.

Then Grandma called and begged me to visit her. I repeated the invitation to Alice to show her somebody cared about me. She immediately latched on to the idea. She said I could use a change; it wasn't good for me to mope around all summer. I said Phoenix was too hot. She said it was dry heat and it couldn't be worse than the weather here. I asked what I'd do in an old people's community. She asked what I was doing here. I worried about leaving Rex. She promised to take care of him.

She said, "I'll fly with you to Phoenix. There's a three-day conference in San Francisco in the middle of August that I'd like to attend. America West flies to San Francisco via Phoenix. We'll travel together and I'll see you safely settled before I go on to San Francisco."

No wonder she was so anxious for me to visit Grandma. She wanted to get rid of me so she could go to her conference. That was fine with me. I wanted to get away from her. "Grandma would never forgive me if I only went for three days."

"If we fly out together, you'll have two weeks to visit before school starts."

"That's not enough. I want to go for all of August. And I don't need you to baby-sit me."

Alice cleared her throat. "I didn't think of it as baby-sitting. However, you're old enough to fly alone if you prefer. It might be a good idea for us to get away from each other for a month."

chapter
17

I went to visit Grandma early in August and stayed until Labor Day. Phoenix was like a different world with mountains and desert all around, cactus in the gardens, baking heat outside, and the steady hum of air-conditioning inside.

Everyone in Grandma's retirement community was old. The only time I saw anyone under sixty was at the mall or when some neighbor's visiting grandchild splashed in the pool. Then the grandchild was usually under six. I was the only teen around, and it made me a kind of celebrity. Grandma's friends all fussed over me. They asked wasn't I afraid of getting mugged living in New York and did I have a boyfriend. They pressed their special chocolate cake and banana nut bread on me. They told Grandma how pretty and smart and well-mannered I was. When they thought I wasn't listening, they added how bravely I handled my tragedy.

Grandma decided I was too thin and insisted on making me French toast, pancakes, or raisin oatmeal for breakfast. After she washed the dishes and cleaned up the kitchen, she browsed through the newspaper and clipped the coupons while I read the new Anne Rice book. Then she cooked my lunch. She made me sit and digest before I went in the pool. When I got bored with swimming, she took me to the mall. Grandma loved shopping. She couldn't resist a bargain. She talked her hairdresser into charging me the special senior rate for a stylish new haircut, and I ended up with enough on-sale blouses and beads and books to last me for years. On shopping days, Grandma treated me to the early-bird dinner at the local restaurant. Then we took in a movie or watched TV and went to bed for "our eight hours of soothing sleep."

It was like relaxing in a warm bath. I gave myself up to being taken care of. I didn't think of anything else. I didn't wonder if Rooji had gotten a chance to act yet or how I could stand living with Alice. Nothing outside Phoenix seemed to exist as August slipped gently by.

chapter
18

A s I came through the gate at Kennedy Airport, the excitement and energy of New York grabbed me. It made me feel alive. I couldn't wait to see Rex and get ready for school and . . .

Alice shouted my name. She pushed through the crowd and hugged me like there had never been any strain between us. I guess it's true that absence makes the heart grow fonder. I found myself smiling and hugging her back.

While we waited at the luggage carousel, she admired my new hairdo and caught me up on the news. She reported that her conference had been great, the washing machine was finally fixed, and Rex was eating well and gaining weight although he missed me. I said Phoenix was very relaxing, Grandma had bought me lots of new clothes, and I was dying to see Rex.

Then, as my suitcase tumbled down the luggage chute, Alice dropped her bomb. "It's not definite yet, but it looks like my trial will be coming up in October."

My suitcase sailed past. I lunged for it. A fat lady blocked me and I missed. Now I had to wait for it to come all the way around again. I struggled to keep my voice steady. "So soon? I read this magazine article about cases taking forever to go to trial."

"I don't know how Erica managed it, but she did. We're hoping that the reporters who covered the protest will also cover the trial."

If the reporters didn't have enough to write about, Alice

could always bop another cop. My suitcase came around. I broke a fingernail down to the quick snagging it.

We got into a cab with a Pakistani driver who didn't speak English and had no idea where Brooklyn was. Alice spent the whole ride trying to direct him. Although I was spared hearing any more about her trial, I couldn't stop thinking about it. October was next month. I tried to tell myself that Alice said the date wasn't definite. I argued that the trial could be postponed. Maybe even more than once. If it was postponed long enough, Alice might even decide not to go through with it. But I couldn't convince myself.

Rex bounded to greet me as I stepped into the house. While I hugged and petted him, Alice sorted through the day's mail. She tossed most of it onto the pile of junk that accumulated on the table near the door. A pile of unread catalogs, torn shopping bags, odd gloves, and . . . I asked, "How did my Indian bangle bracelet get there? I lost it ages ago."

"Jill found it behind her sofa and brought it back."

"Why would Jill come all the way to Brooklyn to return it when she could wait until she saw me in school?"

"When she called about the bracelet—not knowing you were in Phoenix—we got to talking about the protest. Why didn't you tell me Jill was an eyewitness? That she saw exactly what happened?"

I didn't know what Alice was driving at, but it made me nervous. "It never occurred to me."

"Didn't it occur to you that I'd need witnesses at my trial?"

It hadn't. But it did now. A horrible picture flashed through my mind of Jill sharing all the gory details of Alice's trial with the girls at school while I had to sit and listen. I stammered, "Is . . . is that why Jill was here? Is she going to testify at your trial?"

"When Jill told me what she saw, I asked her to come and repeat her story to Erica. Erica thinks Jill would be a valuable witness. Of course she's underage and needs her parents' permission . . ."

I couldn't bear to hear any more. Although I was back in New York for only two hours, I was already desperate to be somewhere else.

●━●━●

The play about the kidnapped prince was ending. It was the same play Rooji and I had seen the day we arrived in London, only now we were watching from backstage. Rooji was about to make her stage debut doing a *dumb show* (mime) after the last scene while the other "ladies" sang.

She clung to my hand as she waited for her entrance. Her fingers were clammy with stage fright. To distract her, I asked, "Did you see the letter Master Bowen wrote to the lord chamberlain?"

"Such fulsome apologies! Master Greene said 'twas not necessary to be quite so humble. He did not like having to add his name as company manager to such a humiliating letter."

"Maybe that's why Master Bowen was so fulsome. Or maybe he was being sarcastic to protest his being treated unfairly."

"Unfairly?"

"There's your cue." I gave her a little shove.

Rooji stepped out onto the stage. She struck a pose and stood still until she had the audience's attention. Then she acted out a pantomime of loyalty and betrayal among the gods on Mount Olympus. She was wonderful. Her movements were so eloquent that you didn't need the ladies' song to follow what she was doing. When she finished and bowed low, the audience clapped and stamped and begged for more. She gave them an encore: a mime of a fine lady being chased by her lapdog that sent them into gales of laughter.

At dinner after the show, the actors congratulated Rooji on her performance. Master Fletcher said she'd handled the train of her costume deftly. Master Greene scolded her for padding her part, but he gave her a speaking role in the next play. Master Bowen did not say or do anything. He was nowhere to be seen.

I was gobbling the last of my stewed *coney* (rabbit) when Master Bowen appeared and whispered in Rooji's ear. She pulled me away from the table hissing, "Hurry! We are in danger!"

I let her drag me behind a pile of boxes and barrels. Then I peeked out and saw three men in black doublets enter and surround Master Bowen. While I watched in horror, they chained his hands behind his back.

After they dragged him out, Rooji moaned, "I caused this by doing the comic turn. I only meant the lady to be a lady. There was no hidden meaning. But I should have known that informers in the audience would be watching to see that Master Bowen kept to the approved script."

"You mustn't blame yourself. You didn't do anything wrong."

She shook her head. "I acted out of vanity. And Master Bowen sacrificed himself for me. If he had not come to warn me, he might have escaped. Now he will rot in prison, and it is all my fault."

I insisted, "Neither you nor Master Bowen did anything wrong."

Too bad I couldn't say the same for Alice. Turning my back on her, I grabbed my suitcase and lugged it to my room. When I opened the door, the Hide-A-Bed, lumpy chair, and scruffy carpet were gone. In their place was all my old furniture: my bed and chest, my beanbag chair, my Mexican area rugs, my framed letters from Judy Blume and Stephen King.

Behind me, Alice said, "Welcome home."

"You sold the apartment!"

Completely misunderstanding, she bragged, "Remember the old lady with the calico cat? Her great-nephew in Ohio was transferred to New York and needed an apartment right away. He paid our full asking price. Enough to send you to any college you want when you're ready."

"I don't care what he paid. I don't care about college. How could you sell my home behind my back? How could you!"

She looked like I'd slapped her. "It wasn't behind your back. You knew the apartment had to be sold—although you wouldn't discuss it. Since you found the idea painful, I decided not to disturb your Phoenix vacation when the offer came. I thought that this," she gestured at the redone room, "would make it easier for you."

Although I knew she was telling the truth (she always told the truth even when you didn't want to hear it), I couldn't forgive her for what she'd done. "What did you do with Mom and Dad's furniture and clothes and stuff? Throw them in the garbage?"

Her temper flared. "Don't speak to me like that! I am your guardian and I expect you to treat me with respect."

My parents had been big on respect. I automatically hung my head and muttered, "I'm sorry."

Alice immediately switched back to her let's-be-buddies routine. "Lisa, I know you're grieving and I am, too, but . . ."

I cut her off firmly. "I was out of line and I apologize."

She cleared her throat, started to say something, and then changed her mind. "All right. Apology accepted. Do you need help unpacking?"

"No, thank you."

She left. I closed the door behind her and sank into my beanbag chair. I was too tired to unpack.

I was still sitting there when Alice knocked on the door. She said "Call for you," and handed me the phone. She left without bothering to tell me who was calling.

Brian didn't bother to say "Hello" or to apologize for walking out on me when the hypnosis didn't work. He announced, "I'm back from the country. And I'm finished with your report on Elizabethan theaters. Want me to drop it over?"

"What are you doing with my English report?"

"I asked Alice to lend it to me."

Alice had been a busy beaver while I was in Phoenix. Jill, the apartment, and now Brian. "Bring it back this minute."

Brian took his own sweet time coming over. I checked my report for chocolate or jelly stains before I asked, "What did you want this for?"

He gave me a typical Brian answer. "There's nothing in your report you couldn't have found in the library."

"Okay. Don't tell me. I'm not interested."

"You should be interested."

"Well, I'm not."

To be contrary, he told me. "There's nothing much to do in the country on rainy days. I got to thinking about why I couldn't go back to the past with you. So I studied the lists we made again. Do you know what I came up with?"

"I don't want to know. I've had a horrible day. I'm tired and I'm not in the mood for your theories."

That didn't stop him. He said, "What I discovered is that you go back to Rooji when you're upset about something."

"So what? Even if you're right, what difference does that make?"

I should never have asked. He said triumphantly, "My theory is that when something really bugs you, you try to run away from it. You imagine that you go back into the past, and that makes you feel better."

"That's the stupidest thing I ever heard. I was with Rooji not an hour ago. She got her first acting role, and Master Bowen was arrested because she padded her part."

"What made you go back this time? Did something here upset you?"

I'd been crazy to ever tell him about Rooji. My only excuse was that I'd been so shocked and dazed by the crash that I'd latched on to the first person who came along—even if he was stupid and obnoxious. Well, I'd learned my lesson now. "Believe what you want. I don't want to talk about it. Just go home and leave me alone."

He hung around, trying to draw me into discussing his theory. I refused to say a word. I opened my suitcase and started to unpack. Alice had stuffed the clothes I left behind into the wrong drawers. I moved the underwear to the top drawer where it belonged. I sorted and folded the T-shirts and put them neatly in the second drawer.

Brian finally got tired of talking to my back and left. As soon as he was gone, I abandoned my task. I was exhausted. I felt like I'd been digging ditches for hours. Leaving the suitcase open on the floor, I lay down on my old comfortable bed. The bed seemed to take me in its arms. I drifted off to sleep.

When I opened my eyes again and saw my familiar furniture, I thought I was back in my old room. Filled with relief and joy, I leapt off the bed to run and tell Mom what a horrible dream I'd had. Then I saw that the room's door and window were in the wrong place. The walls were the wrong color. I remembered where I was, and my joy changed to misery.

The misery hit me like a punch in the stomach. For the past months, I'd been so busy with Rooji's theater and Brian's schemes and being upset with Alice that most of the time I managed to avoid thinking too much about Mom and Dad. I'd done a kind of trick in my mind, not exactly pretending that they'd just gone away for a while, but half believing that what happened was only temporary. Now my loss became horribly final.

If Brian's theory was right, I'd have gone back to Rooji right then. I didn't. I sat on the edge of my bed and let the waves of misery and loneliness wash over me. Misery and loneliness and guilt.

Guilt for being alive. Guilt for not grieving properly.

To ease my guilt, I made a solemn promise to think about Mom and Dad every day. Every morning and every evening and whenever I could in-between. I promised myself I'd remember all the things they had done for me and everything they taught me. I vowed to become the kind of person they had wanted me to be. From now on, before I did anything I'd ask myself: Would Mom approve? What would Dad say? Then I would act the way they wanted.

chapter
19

I tried to keep my promise to remember Mom and Dad every morning and evening. All kinds of things interfered. School started the next day. Because I'd gotten used to sleeping late, I overslept and had to rush out. Guiltily, I promised myself I'd make up the time in the evening.

I did. And I got up early the next morning. But that evening Jill called just as I was settling down to remember. She said she needed the English assignment. She really wanted to talk about Alice's trial, which was the last thing in the world I wanted to hear about, but Jill talked on and on. She told me that her father had said she could be a witness. Now her mother didn't want her to testify. Jill was afraid her mother would convince her father to change his mind. Although I only answered her in grunts, Jill kept talking. By the time she finally hung up, I was too tired to do anything but escape into sleep.

The following evening, Brian came over with some papers his father wanted Alice to give Erica. Mr. Gordon was going to testify at the trial. Brian hung around discussing legal strategy with Alice. I turned on the TV and watched the first thing that came on so I wouldn't have to listen.

As I stared at a stupid sitcom when I should have been thinking about Mom and Dad, I realized that something had to be done. I had to get myself organized. I switched off the TV, went into my room, took a clean page out of my loose-leaf, and started a schedule.

First I listed the things I did every day: school, home-work, walking Rex, eating, sleeping, reading, TV. Then I listed things I did from time to time: chorus (on Tuesdays), library, shopping, dentist. I didn't know where to put Rooji, so I wrote her name on the side. I wrote REMEMBERING MOM AND DAD in capital letters across the top of the page.

I studied the page. Then I crossed off TV. Dad had called TV "the great American time waster." I crossed out shopping. Grandma had bought me enough clothes to last until I was twenty. I hesitated over chorus and reading, but keeping my promise was more important. I drew firm lines through them. Finally, I drew a line through Rooji. Now I was ready.

I developed a routine over the next days. I came home from school, did my homework, and ate. Then I called Rex and hung my DO NOT DISTURB sign on the door to my room. I curled up on the bed, hugged Rex to me, and remembered the way it used to be with Mom and Dad. After a while, tears would start dripping out of my eyes onto Rex's fur.

I was careful not to let Brian or Jill interfere with my withdrawal into grief. When Brian came over, I said I had homework to do. He shrugged and went in to Alice to hear what was happening with the trial. He really had more to talk about to Alice than to me. Since I refused to discuss either the trial or going back to the past, we had nothing to say to each other.

When Jill did her will-my-parents-let-me-testify routine at lunch, I hid behind a book or went to the bathroom. When she called me at home, I made excuses not to talk. It was a relief when her parents' final answer was "No." Then Jill insisted on coming to Brooklyn on Saturday to "study." I forgot she was coming and went to the library—leaving her to get the gossip from Alice, which was what she really wanted. Jill's feelings were hurt. After that, she left me alone.

Getting rid of Brian and Jill was easy once I'd made up my mind. I expected Alice to be harder. Mom would've asked what I was doing locked up in my room so much. Mom would've said I was getting to look like the underside of a mushroom. (I looked in the mirror; my face was pale.) Mom would've told me to go out and enjoy the glorious weather. (We were having perfect sunny September days.)

Alice didn't do any of those things. She didn't notice how long I was in my room or how many soggy tissues were stuffed in my wastebasket. She was too busy gabbing on the phone with Erica or with some guy named Vernon she'd met at her conference. He was a vet in the Bronx. When Alice went to meet him in Manhattan, she always asked if I minded staying alone. I always said I had plenty to do. She never asked what.

When Alice wasn't on the phone or out with Vernon and I wasn't holed up in my room, we got along okay. It was like my grieving for Mom and Dad made it easier for me to stand Alice. Especially since she respected my refusal to discuss the trial. We talked about Rex's diet and Bathsheba's jealousy and whether Dr. Sung would move to California.

Alice only mentioned the trial once. One evening toward the end of September, while we were eating vegetarian Chinese takeout straight from the cartons, she said, "My trial date is set for October thirteenth."

I said, "I'll make a note of it," and changed the subject. "I'm glad I have Ms. Surowitz for English again. She works us hard, but she makes the books come alive."

"Maybe she's working you too hard. You don't seem to have time for anything but homework."

I was surprised she'd noticed. I said, "I like the challenge." Then I dropped my carton in the garbage and went into my room. I didn't call Rex to come with me. He'd gotten impatient with my crying on his shoulder. He wanted to play instead. So I had to manage without him.

The tears didn't come as easily without Rex to hug. Sometimes my mind wandered. I'd suddenly realize that I'd been wondering what Rooji was doing and what had happened to Master Bowen. Then I'd force my thoughts back to my grief. Grieving can be exhausting. Sometimes, to my shame and guilt, I'd doze off.

I was sound asleep when Alice came into my room one night. She shook me awake. "I saw the light under your door and knocked, but you didn't hear me. Now I find you asleep fully dressed. Are you all right?"

I muttered, "I'm fine. I just dozed off doing my homework." Then I realized that all my schoolbooks were stacked neatly on my desk.

Alice didn't notice where my books were. She said, "I hope you're not getting sick with my trial starting next week."

"Don't worry. My health won't interfere with the trial."

"You know I didn't mean it that way."

I didn't answer. I stared at the wall to show that the subject was closed.

She didn't take the hint. "The reason I came in is that I need to talk to you about the trial."

I examined my fingernails. They needed to be cut.

She cleared her throat. "Were you planning to be at my trial?"

The question caught me unprepared. I'd avoided it until now by not talking or thinking about the trial. I stalled. "Do I have a choice?"

"Yes, you do have a choice. Erica and I argued about it. Erica insists on my making a good impression on the jury: having my hair done, wearing a dress, and so on. I went along until she said that juries form favorable opinions of defendants whose families are in court supporting them. You're all the family I have left, and Erica wants you there to remind the jury why I acted as I did. I insisted I wanted to win the case on its merits, not play up to the jury. She told me to let her do her job. I said, 'Not if it means sneaky lawyer tricks.' She said I was stubborn and stupid. When we calmed down, I agreed to a haircut and a skirt and she agreed to let you decide if you wanted to attend the trial."

Erica was right: Alice was stupid and stubborn. I wouldn't put it past her to show up at the trial in her tatty old jeans. At least I didn't have to be there to see it. I could tell her that I couldn't skip school. If she—and the jury—guessed that I was staying away because I disapproved of what Alice had done, that wasn't my responsibility.

Or was it? I'd made myself two promises. The first was to remember Mom and Dad. The second was to act the way they would want me to. I'd kept my first promise. Maybe not perfectly, but I'd done my best. Now I had to keep my second promise. I asked myself what my parents would think of me if Alice went to jail because I was ashamed to show up in court.

I heard Mom's voice in my head saying, "You are responsible for your actions."

Before I could chicken out, I said, "Erica is right about making a good impression on the jury. Of course I'll be at the trial. Ask Erica to give me a note for school. And ask her what I should wear."

chapter
20

I sat in the courtroom dressed in the pleated skirt and navy blazer Grandma had bought me on sale. The cop that Alice hit was testifying. I tried to seem supportive of Alice, but I could feel my face growing hot with shame. At least the reporters hadn't come. They were all at the big murder trial that filled the news.

I didn't know where to look. I couldn't bear to watch the prosecutor encouraging the cop to describe "the defendant's unprovoked attack." Watching the court stenographer tap his damning words into a little machine was no better. I was afraid to look at the jury. I'd die if I discovered them staring at me. So I looked down at the floor until I remembered Erica warning me against doing that. Then I sat up straight and fixed my eyes on the clock on the wall.

After what seemed like hours, although the minute hand hardly moved, I peeked at Alice. In her Liz Claiborne dress, with her hair done and her face made up, she didn't look like somebody who would deliberately bop a cop over the head. But the cop and the prosecutor and the millions of people who had seen her on TV knew better. So what good did her dressing up do? What good was my sitting in court like a statue of a loyal niece?

Brian dropped into the seat next to me. "How's it going?"

"Awful. The cop is making Alice sound like the Wicked Witch of the West." I turned to him, "Why aren't you in school?"

"I cut out after my first period math test. No way I'd miss this."

"It isn't a show for your amusement. Alice is charged with assault in the second degree, disorderly conduct, and obstruction of justice!"

"Don't make it sound like high treason. Assault is the only thing that matters. The reason Erica didn't get the other charges dismissed is that assault carries a mandatory jail sentence and the others don't. In case the jury gets in a convicting mood, Erica's giving them less serious charges to consider."

"Shh. I want to hear her cross examination."

I would have been better off not hearing. Erica couldn't shake the cop's story. No, he insisted, he hadn't done anything to provoke Alice. No, he hadn't used undue force on the college kids. He wasn't even the one who had arrested them.

The prosecution called the arresting officers next. They backed up the first cop's story and made Alice look totally depraved. I forced myself to hold my shoulders back and my head high. Mom used to say that proper posture gave one confidence while it made a good impression on others. It didn't work for me. My back muscles just knotted and my jaw ached from gritting my teeth to hide my shame and anger.

When the judge finally announced the lunch break, I headed straight for the door. Brian stopped at the table where Alice and Erica were sitting. He said the trial seemed to be going okay and they agreed. Alice told him to wait until our turn at bat. He said he was looking forward to it. Were they both crazy?

I interrupted, "Brian and I are going for burgers." I yanked at his sleeve to get him moving before Alice could suggest our going with her to some restaurant that served seaweed sandwiches.

Alice said, "Erica wants to review her notes with me, so

we'll send out for salads. But I'll treat you." She pawed through the mess in her bag and handed me a twenty. "This is too much." I don't know why she made me feel guilty. I hadn't done anything wrong. I wasn't on trial. "Gorge yourselves. It's going to be a long afternoon." Why did she have to remind me? I pocketed the money and turned to go. Before I could make my escape, some skinny guy I didn't know came hurrying over. He apologized for not being able to get there earlier and Alice said she was glad he'd come. She introduced him. "Lisa, this is Vernon. Vernon gave a paper on animal rights at the conference I went to in San Francisco."

I said, "Pleased to meet you." At that moment I wouldn't have been pleased to meet Tom Cruise. I just wanted to get out of there. I sneaked away while Alice was catching Vernon up on the morning's testimony.

The afternoon didn't start off as awful as I expected. When I returned to court, stuffed with a double cheeseburger, large fries, and a thick shake, the prosecution called eyewitnesses to Alice's hitting the cop. None of them had seen what happened earlier. In her cross-examination, Erica made them admit that it was possible that Alice was protecting the college kids or, at least, that she believed she was.

I'd never seen anything like the way Erica led the witnesses into saying what she wanted. It was as if she was playing a game she was an expert at and was determined to win. As she scored one point after another, I began to believe that she might just pull it off. I stopped hanging on each word as if everything depended on my agonizing.

I deserved a little break, and all that food was making me drowsy. I leaned back and relaxed. My mind wandered.

A kung fu yell jolted me into full awareness. The prosecution was showing the videotape of the protest. In the video Alice seemed to look directly at me as she raised her protest sign.

Instinctively, I turned away before the sign struck—and met the eyes of a middle-aged woman in the first row of the jury. She looked as horrified as I felt. Whatever hope I'd had was dashed. Erica could play her clever games, but this responsible woman would never forgive Alice for enjoying her irresponsible act. She would convince the other jurors to send Alice to jail.

○●○

I jumped to my feet to avoid the woman's eyes. But there were no women on the jury. No Asian- or African-Americans. Everyone in court was a white man except Rooji and me, and we were in disguise.

Rooji clutched my sleeve. "We must not lose our places. Master Bowen's trial is after this one."

While we waited, I looked around curiously. Three red-robed judges sat on carved wooden chairs in front of the room. Twelve jurors were crammed together on a narrow bench along the side. The defendant, witnesses, and lawyers stood, as did the crowd of spectators in back of the room. The witnesses testified, the judges asked questions, and the clerks wrote everything down. I was surprised at how similar it was to Alice's trial.

The defendant made a speech insisting on his innocence. (Would Alice speak in her own defense? What could she say after that video?) Then the chief judge summed up the case for the jury.

I complained to Rooji, "The judge practically told the jury to convict the defendant!"

She asked, "How else would they know how to vote?" It wasn't as much like a modern trial as I'd thought.

The jury returned with the verdict: "Guilty, my lords." The judges consulted one another. Then the chief judge pronounced sentence, "The criminal shall be taken to the marketplace one week hence where his ears shall be chopped off."

Horrified, I turned to Rooji. "They won't do anything like that to Master Bowen, will they? He just broke some stupid rule."

She looked miserable. "If Master Bowen is charged with disobeying the lord chamberlain, he will be fined and sentenced to the time he has already spent in prison. If the charge is treason . . ."

"You still don't know what he's accused of! How can his lawyer prepare a defense?"

"Master Bowen will defend himself. And Master Greene went to beg the duke to use his influence for the lesser charge. Unfortunately, the duke had left for his estate in Kent. Master Greene set out after the duke. He has not yet returned."

I felt sick to my stomach. I didn't have to ask Rooji what the punishment for treason was. I'd seen the heads stuck up on pikes on London Bridge.

The jailers led out the defendant who was doomed to lose his ears. Master Bowen was brought in. An official in a gold-laced gown unrolled a document and began to read the *bill of complaint* against Master Bowen.

● ● ●

The last prosecution witness stepped down. Erica stood up and addressed the judge. She said that the evidence was all prejudiced or weak. Erica asked the judge to dismiss the charges against Alice.

"Motion denied. Court will adjourn until nine tomorrow morning when the defense will present its case."

I looked at the woman in the first row of the jury. She looked back as if to say, "What defense could there possibly be?"

chapter
21

Erica called character witnesses for the defense. Dr. Sung testified that Alice was an excellent veterinarian. The old lady who owned the calico cat said that Alice really cared about her patients. The director of Pets for Sick Children praised Alice's volunteer work for his organization. Other witnesses declared that she was honest, hardworking, and bothered by injustice. It was all true (although I hadn't known about the volunteer work). But what was the point? Alice wasn't accused of lying or laziness. She was on trial for assaulting a cop.

After each witness, the prosecutor said, "No questions."

Brian took the seat I'd saved for him. "My dad is next."

Mr. Gordon took the oath. Erica asked him about the relatives' group. She led him gently through their losses and grief and their determination that others should not suffer as they had. I sneaked a glance at the woman in the first row of the jury. She looked like she was going to cry. Good work, Erica.

After Mr. Gordon told about the group's struggle to get the airlines to pay attention, Erica asked, "Whose idea was the protest?"

"Mine. However, Alice Markham organized it."

"Why was that?"

"She volunteered. She was angry about the lack of security at the airports."

"Any other reason?"

"She told us that she needed to do something constructive

with her grief. She wanted the protest to be a memorial to her sister, to make her sister proud of her."

I couldn't believe my ears. How could Alice possibly imagine that Mom would be proud of her horrible behavior? Erica asked, "Did Dr. Markham do a good job of organizing the protest?"

"Yes. She devoted a great deal of time and effort to it." He described Alice's each-one-reach-one telephone chain and her publicity campaign. While he was telling how hard she'd worked, I was asking myself, "Then why did she go and ruin it?"

This time the prosecutor had questions. "You said that Alice Markham threw herself wholeheartedly into the protest to deal with her grief. Did you suspect that because of her emotional state the protest was too important to her, that her judgment was impaired, that she might act irrationally?"

Erica objected.

Although the judge told the jury to ignore the prosecutor's last question, I saw that it had scored with the juror in the first row.

Erica's next two witnesses were the college guys Alice had rescued. They said they'd felt threatened by the cops and frightened of going to jail. But under cross-examination they had to admit that the cops hadn't really hurt them. They also admitted that, because they were facing the police car, they hadn't actually seen Alice confront the cop. I hoped Erica knew what she was doing.

Erica called a relative to confirm that he'd taped the protest to use for publicity. Then she prepared to show his videotape.

I turned to Brian. "Wasn't the first video bad enough? How can Erica be so dumb?"

"Give her a chance."

"I did. I mean, I am."

"You never give people a real chance. One strike and they're out."

"That's so ridiculous I won't dignify it with an answer."

"Sure. Hide behind your holier-than-thou silence."

I didn't answer. The video started. There were pans of the crowd and close-ups of protesters waving their signs. There were shots of the airline office, the snarled traffic, and the police cars.

Erica pressed the PAUSE button and described the picture on the screen. "Officers are pushing the previous witnesses into a police car. The witnesses testified that they were frightened, as you can clearly see in their faces. You can also clearly see how menacing the officers' behavior would look to someone coming onto the scene."

I could see what Erica meant, but I couldn't see it *clearly*.

She continued, "Unfortunately the camera's view was blocked at this point. However, the next witness can describe exactly what happened. The defense calls Alice Markham."

◐◦◑

Master Bowen stepped forward. His voice rang out as it did onstage. "If I have offended against any law or any official of the queen's government, I am truly sorry."

"Good opening," Master Greene said like he was judging a new play. All the Duke's Men were in the courtroom. I wanted to ask Master Greene if he'd reached the duke and what the duke had said, but a helper doesn't dare speak to the company manager unless spoken to.

Master Bowen proclaimed, "Whatever my fault, I would rather die than do anything to hurt my queen or my country."

Master Greene said, "He need not remind the court that it has the power to sentence him to death."

Master Bowen went on, "I adore her exalted majesty, Queen Elizabeth, and I bleed when false advice leads her to act against the perfection of her nature."

"Fool!" snapped Master Greene.

Rooji whispered to me, "What can possess Master Bowen

to remind the court of the witch speech after he has been pardoned for it?"

I'd learned something about conducting a defense from watching Erica. "Give him a chance. If the queen got bad advice about the taxes, then Master Bowen was right to . . ."

"He wasn't right!" Rooji insisted so loudly that Master Greene threw her an angry look. It showed how strongly she felt that she didn't immediately fall silent. She whispered, "It is a crime to criticize the queen. It is treason."

I whispered back, "Because it's against the law doesn't make it wrong. Sometimes laws are wrong and someone has to challenge them."

"Hush! Master Greene is glaring at us."

<hr>

There was a hush as Alice took the witness stand. She was wearing the baggy old gray suit she'd adopted for Thanksgiving dinners after Mom lectured her about coming in jeans. And she'd wrecked her fancy blow-dry by raking her fingers through her hair. Her appearance announced that she didn't intend to play up to the jury. When she swore to tell the truth, the whole truth, and nothing but the truth, I knew she would do exactly that no matter what the consequences. In another time and place, I might have admired her honesty.

Alice described how the plane crash changed her life. She spoke simply and honestly about needing to do something with her grief. I was reminded of the lovely interview that never made the TV news. The juror in the first row listened carefully.

Erica asked, "Were you close to your sister?"

"We loved each other, but when we were together we usually ended up arguing. She didn't approve of me. She thought I was irresponsible."

Erica frowned like she hadn't expected that answer. (Why did Alice have to be *so* truthful?) Then Erica said smoothly,

"Your sister clearly didn't think you were too irresponsible to be her daughter's guardian."

Alice looked like she'd never thought of it that way before. "That's so, isn't it? When she was planning her will, my sister intended to make her friend in Chicago Lisa's guardian. She changed her mind after I offered."

"Why did you offer to be your niece's guardian?"

Alice said, like it was obvious, "It was the right thing to do."

Erica asked, "Do you always try to do the right thing? Even when it is difficult or it might get you into trouble?"

Alice answered, "I try to follow my conscience."

The juror in the first row looked thoughtful. I felt thoughtful, too. "Follow your conscience" was one of the rules Mom tried to teach me. Maybe Alice wasn't as totally different from Mom as I'd imagined.

I reminded myself that Mom would never bop a cop. Not unless the cop was actually hitting a helpless old person or beating up somebody in a wheelchair or . . .

Someone was pushing into our row and making everyone move over. Annoyed, I turned and saw Vernon. Why couldn't he come on time? Why had he come at all?

Alice was explaining, "Since the protest was a memorial to my sister, I did it her way. I applied for a permit, dug through the endless red tape, and tried to be patient when I was put on hold and forgotten. I did everything by the book until I saw the police hassling the boys. Then I had to stop them in any way I could."

❦

The judge asked Master Bowen, "You were faulted once for changing a play after the censors approved it. Why did you not learn from your error? Why did you add to the dumb show?"

Master Bowen insisted, "There was no offense in the dumb show."

The judge said severely, "It was not your place to decide."

Master Bowen did not argue. Neither did he apologize.

Rooji moaned, "He is damning himself for something he did not do." I had to hold on to her doublet to keep her from running up to interfere.

⬤⬤⬤

Brian pulled me back into my seat. I moaned, "Alice practically admitted hitting the cop. How could she do that? How could Erica let her do that?"

Brian said, "Give them a chance."

Erica asked Alice, "Why did you think the action you took was necessary?"

"To protect two innocent young men. Unfortunately, the police tend to think the worst of boys who wear earrings and have nonregulation haircuts. The police decided—without any evidence—that the boys were troublemakers. Since they wouldn't listen to reason, I stopped reasoning." She added, like it explained everything, "As organizer of the protest, I was responsible for the boys' safety."

"Did you fear for their safety?"

"I didn't expect the cops to beat them bloody, but being shoved into a police car is bad enough. And having a police record when you're starting out in life is worse. It was my responsibility to protect them from that."

It made an Alice kind of sense. Would the jury buy it?

⬤⬤⬤

The men of the jury looked puzzled when Master Bowen said there was a larger issue at stake than one play and one playwright.

Rooji was puzzled, too. She whispered to me, "What does Master Bowen mean by 'freedom of speech'?"

I didn't know how to explain it to her. I whispered back, "He'll tell us. Just listen."

Master Bowen made a splendid poetic speech, better than

anything he'd ever written for a play. He said it was the right and responsibility of the playwright, indeed the right and responsibility of every man, to think for himself and to speak out against injustice. He said that in his time men had to speak softly, but the day would come when they could speak out boldly.

He delivered his words in his ringing actor's voice and punctuated them with his grand actor's gestures. As I listened spellbound, I had the feeling I'd heard a similar speech somewhere before. Then I remembered the tape we saw of Martin Luther King's "I have a dream" speech when we learned about civil rights in school. Behind the flowery Elizabethan phrases, Master Bowen was saying the same thing— that he had a dream of a better, fairer world.

I whispered to Rooji. "Isn't he wonderful?"

Rooji looked shocked.

●━◐━●

The prosecutor cross-examined Alice. "If you were in the same situation again, would you still strike the officer?"

Erica objected, but Alice said she would like to answer.

I held my breath. Lie, I prayed. For once in your life do the sensible thing.

Alice said slowly, "I hope that I would be wise enough to find a better way to free the boys."

I went limp with relief. Strangely, I was also disappointed. Which didn't make any sense. Alice had done what I wanted. She'd probably saved herself from jail. Why did I feel let down?

The prosecutor persisted. "What if you couldn't find a better way?"

Alice declared, "Then I would hit the cop."

●━◐━●

The red-robed judge charged the twelve-man jury. "As a playwright, Master Bowen loves the sound of his own words.

Ignore his rhetoric and make your decision on the charge: Did he disobey the necessary rules governing the censorship of plays?"

◗◗◗

The black-robed judge explained the differences between assault, disorderly conduct, and obstruction of justice to the men and women of the jury. She told them to judge each charge separately and to be sure of their verdict "beyond a reasonable doubt."

chapter
22

Elizabethan juries worked fast, but not fast enough for Rooji. She got herself all worked up before they were out ten minutes. She demanded, "Why did Master Bowen make that strange speech? How could he risk the judges' anger after the duke used his influence with them? Surely he realized that the duke would not lift a finger to save him if the judges decided that his speech was treason."

I said, "Then it took great courage for him to speak up for what he believes in."

She shook her head. "His courage—as you call it—comes from pride and arrogance. If Master Bowen's head ends up on a pike on London Bridge, it will be because he stubbornly refuses to accept the rightful judgment of those above him."

Annoyed at *her* stubbornness, I snapped, "If Master Bowen loses his head, I suppose you'll say that it serves him right."

Rooji looked like I'd smacked her. I was immediately sorry. She'd been brought up to believe that the people on top made the rules and it was the duty of the people underneath to obey them. How could I expect her to understand that Master Bowen had a right to think for himself and to speak his mind? Besides, she was blaming Master Bowen to deal with her own guilt. She was angry at him because she was afraid for him.

I said, "Let's not quarrel. Waiting is hard enough."

Modern juries take forever. Brian, his father, Erica, Vernon, Alice, and I went out to lunch. Vernon pushed for some health food place, Brian wanted a burger, and Mr. Gordon said he didn't care what we ate as long as it was fast because he had to get back to work. Erica said she knew a place nearby that would satisfy all of us. The food was good, but Vernon didn't look satisfied. He sniffed at his bean salad like he was afraid someone had slipped broiled toads into it.

I was too nervous to eat much. Alice left most of her food, too, but that was probably because she was busy rehashing the trial with Vernon. Mr. Gordon finished quickly and left for work. Erica went to file some papers. Vernon said he'd stay a while. He changed his mind when Alice said that Erica predicted the verdict would take hours. Brian surprised me by saying he might as well hang around anyway.

Alice, Brian, and I waited in a stuffy, dingy room. I tried to make conversation about anything except the trial. I chattered about clothes and school and books I'd read. Alice gave me one-word answers and flipped through the tattered magazines on the table. Brian produced a pocket computer game and pinged away. I stopped talking.

The minutes dragged by like centuries. I was grateful when Brian offered me a turn at his game. I lost five times in a row. Then I went out to the soda machine for a Coke I didn't want. There were three empty soda cans in front of me by the time Erica finally came in and told us that the jury was back.

●—●—●

The jury declared Master Bowen guilty of breaking the censorship rules. The judges fined him £200, which Master Greene produced on the spot. Master Bowen was released to the congratulations and backslapping of his fellow actors.

As they left the court, the actors discussed what play to use to reopen the theater. Master Greene said Master Bowen should write a new play. One with a trial scene. The other actors clustered around Master Bowen making suggestions. I couldn't get close enough to tell him how impressed I'd been with his speech.

I caught up with Rooji outside of the court. She was talking to a boy actor who usually lorded it over us. When she looked up and saw me, she exclaimed, "Clarence has just given me the most wonderful news! He overheard Master Greene talking to Master Fletcher this morning. Master Greene said if all went well at the trial and the theater reopened, he would promote me from helper to boy actor. This is a great day for me. I am finally becoming a real actor."

I hugged her. "That's marvelous. You'll be a great actor. Just be careful not to 'saw the air with your hands' or 'tear a passion to tatters.' "

"What clever advice." Without giving me a chance to tell her that Shakespeare had said it first, she asked, "You mean like Master Durward?" She did such a wonderful imitation of the company's hammiest actor that Clarence and I burst into fits of giggles. Our laughter spurred her to more imitations, which made us laugh harder. I laughed until I doubled over with a stitch in my side.

Master Fletcher spotted us and called. "Enough foolery. Come along now, boys."

Rooji and Clarence stifled their giggles and ran. I clutched my side and gasped, "Wait for me."

Rooji didn't hear me. She kept going.

When I caught my breath, I took a few steps after her. Then something stopped me. I was happy that Rooji's dream of being an actor was coming true. But I didn't want to be an actor. And I certainly didn't want to spend my life fetching and carrying for an acting company. I wished that Rooji and I could always be together the way we had been when we were little. But we'd grown up to be different people. I wished I could stay to see her act in Master Bowen's new play. But there were things I had to do in my own world.

As I stood there, not able to make up my mind to run after her, not quite ready to let her go, a strange thing happened. Although she hadn't really gone very far, I seemed to be seeing her from a great distance. Rooji seemed to blur, like I was looking at her through the kind of old window glass that makes everything appear wavy and far away.

I'd spent enough time in Elizabethan England to believe—at least a little—in magic signs and omens. This was an omen if I'd ever seen one. I stood motionless and watched Rooji disappear into the crowd. I caught a last glimpse of her coppery hair gleaming in the sun. Then she was gone.

I stood alone for a while. Then I brushed away the tears that had gathered in my eyes. I willed myself into the present where Alice was about to face her jury's verdict.

◗◗◗

Erica and Brian headed to the courtroom. Alice turned around in the waiting room doorway and asked me, "Are you coming?"

I'd been desperate to get out of that suffocating room. Now I wanted to cling to it like a warm bed on a cold morning. I answered, "I'm your niece. How would it look if I wasn't there for the verdict?"

"You don't have to worry about appearances anymore. The jury has made up its mind."

"I didn't mean it that way." I did and I didn't. "I guess I'm scared."

"I'll tell you a secret if you won't tell anyone. I'm scared, too."

She meant to reassure me. Instead she gave me a responsibility I didn't want. If she was scared, I couldn't let her face the jury alone. But I couldn't bear to face them when I believed that Alice had only herself to blame if her head ended up on a pike. Or did I believe it? I was totally confused.

Alice said, "I understand if you'd rather wait here."

"I don't want to stay here." I didn't know what I wanted. My thoughts went round and round, chasing their tails and getting nowhere.

Then I remembered my English teacher making us do free-writing exercises and telling us about a famous writer who said, "How do I know what I think until I see what I say?" I never got the hang of free writing. I always outlined before I wrote and thought before I spoke. But I was ready to try anything. I pretended I was going to free write. I took a few breaths to clear my mind. I opened my mouth. For a minute, I stood there like I was retarded.

Then the words came pouring out. I told Alice, "I don't agree with what you did. I think it was childish and stupid and it embarrassed me terribly. But I have to respect your following your conscience and doing what you thought was right. If I was on the jury, I'd take that into account."

Alice looked surprised. (I was pretty surprised myself.) Then she smiled as if I'd given her a fancy gift-wrapped package. "Thank you. I appreciate your telling me."

chapter
23

The jury found Alice innocent of assault and obstructing justice, but guilty of disturbing the peace. The judge sentenced her to a hundred hours of community service in an animal shelter.

Once it was all safely settled, I didn't mind discussing the trial and the verdict with the girls in the school cafeteria. It was kind of fun being the one in the know. Or it would have been fun if Jill hadn't gone out of her way to contradict everything I said.

I told the girls that the verdict was the jury's way of telling Alice that they sympathized with her motives but she had to learn that some behavior would not be tolerated. Jill asked how I knew what the jury was thinking. She insisted that Alice should have gotten off completely, that the judge shouldn't have punished her. I pointed out that the community service was hardly punishment because Alice had been meaning to help out at the shelter. Jill said that was beside the point.

I told the girls, "You'd think Alice would've had it with the relatives' group. But now she's pushing them to go to Washington and lobby Congress for airline safety laws. She's talking about hiring buses and getting everyone's friends and neighbors to go along. This Vernon guy she's seeing did that with his animal rights society. Alice can't bear to let anyone be more far out than she is."

Jill demanded, "What's far out about lobbying your Congressperson? It's a citizen's right and responsibility. You just think if Alice does it, it's automatically wrong. You'd probably have agreed with the jury if they'd sent her to jail."

That was totally unfair. Stung, I replied, "No thanks to you that Alice didn't go to jail. You talk about what a hero she is, but I didn't see you testifying at her trial."

"You know my parents wouldn't let me."

"Then shut your big mouth!"

The girls all stared at me. They'd never seen me lose my temper before. I apologized. "I didn't mean to yell. Maybe living with Alice is rubbing off on me."

Jill sighed. "Maybe I don't have a right to talk if I didn't have the guts to testify."

Figuring she was pulling a look-how-miserable-you-made-me, I said, "Don't be silly. You couldn't testify without your parents' approval."

Jill fiddled with her milk container. Next she'd run and hide in the bathroom and leave me sitting there feeling guilty.

She didn't. She waited until the other girls were busy discussing the new math teacher. Then she told me in a low voice, "I was secretly glad my parents said I couldn't be a witness. I was scared the lawyers would mix me up and I'd say the wrong thing and Alice would go to jail because of me."

Now I did feel guilty. I told her, "We were all scared. I know I was. And while we were waiting for the verdict, Alice told me she was scared, too."

"You're not just saying that to make me feel better?"

"I swear it's true."

"Then I'm glad I told you. I almost didn't. We used to be good friends, but lately . . ."

Good friends? Although we ate lunch and studied together, I'd never thought of Jill as a good friend. We didn't have fun together or get into long talks or help each other when we were in trouble the way Rooji and I did. Jill had called after Mom and Dad died, but I'd thought . . .

Before I could figure out what I'd thought, Jill went on, "Lately you either don't want to know me or you argue with everything I say."

That was ridiculous. I said, "*I* argue with *you*! *You* always disagree with *me*."

"Is that so? Remember when we were talking about the big murder trial on the news and I said I was sure he hadn't done it? Who told me if I believed that I'd believe any- thing?"

"You're making a big deal out of one little remark. Am I supposed to agree with whatever you say so you'll be my friend?"

Jill rolled up her eyes in a heaven-give-me-patience expres- sion. "This may come as news to you, but people can have dif- ferent ideas and still be friends. Unless one of them always sulks or runs away when you don't totally agree with her."

"I can't help feeling bad when people don't like me."

"Then you shouldn't make it hard for people to go on liking you. You shouldn't let them travel all the way to Brooklyn to see you and then 'forget' they're coming."

I knew she'd throw that up to me sooner or later. I was tempted to argue that she'd really come to get the gossip from Alice, not to see me. But I couldn't do it. I said, "I'm sorry about that. I was grieving for my parents, and I just couldn't face anyone."

"Why didn't you tell me how you felt? I would've under- stood. Why do you always keep everything to yourself?"

I had to admit, "I don't know."

We didn't say anything for a while. Finally I offered, "I'm still grieving, but not all the time like I was. If you'll come to Brooklyn again, we can go shopping. Seventh Avenue has these trendy little shops and an ice-cream parlor that makes its own whipped cream. I'll treat you to an ice-cream soda to make up for last time."

"How about Saturday?"

"Great."

"Should we ask Melinda to come, too?"

"Sure. But she has to buy her own soda."

It was hard to believe that we'd gone from fighting to friendship in a few minutes. Maybe there was something to be said for not keeping your feelings to yourself.

●━●━●

Although my time sense had improved, when I marked the appointment with Jill and Melinda on my wall calendar, I was surprised to see that it was nearly six months since the plane crash. To honor the half-year anniversary of Mom and Dad's death, I locked myself in my room with Rex and had a good cry. I'd gotten out of the habit of nightly grieving since the trial interrupted it, but I didn't feel guilty. I remembered Mom and Dad at odd times. Sometimes I hardly thought of them for days. Then something would remind me and I'd almost burst into tears in the middle of the street. That would probably keep happening for a long, long time.

I was beginning to realize that a lot of things were going to stay the way they were for a long, long time. Like living with Alice.

Jill had said that I thought everything Alice did was wrong even if it wasn't. Maybe Jill was right, but I wondered how tolerant she'd be if she had to live with Alice. Alice's lifestyle was the complete opposite of the sane and orderly way I'd lived with Mom and Dad. Alice had no patience with order, routine, or thinking things out. She was into horrible housekeeping, weird ideas, and snap decisions.

I tried not to let it get to me. I told myself that I was stuck with her until I was old enough to go away to college. That just made it worse. Every little thing got on my nerves. I told myself to concentrate on Alice's good points, but it was hard to think of any. I gritted my teeth and kept my mouth shut while the pressure built up in my head.

One evening the dam burst. I told Alice that the yogurt salad dressing smelled like babies' spit-up. I said the whole house smelled. Once I got started, I couldn't stop. I complained that the beds hadn't been changed in weeks. I said when I went to change my own bed, there were no clean sheets. Or towels, either. I pointed out the disgusting state of the bathroom. I detailed the lack of edible food and the mess everywhere. I kept it up until Alice lost her temper and called me an "insufferable little prig." I lost mine right back and declared I'd rather be a prig than a pig like her.

It was a relief to let myself go. It was also kind of fun, like when Ned traded insults with the 'prentices in The Theatre. I was about to call her a "puerile poxied pig" when she marched out of the room.

She came back with a large pad and a freshly sharpened pencil. "Here. List the household chores you think need to be done."

I went to work with a will. I wrote until the pencil point was worn down. Alice read through my list. "Okay. Let's divvy this up."

"What?"

"Roommates often draw up housework contracts to save fighting and resentment. They divide the chores and decide who should do what."

That was definitely not what I'd had in mind. She wasn't my roommate. She was my aunt, and I wanted her to act like one. I stammered, "But . . ."

"But what?" When I didn't answer, she answered for me. "But you don't want to do anything. You just want me to live by your standards."

I tried the when-you're-on-the-spot-put-the-other-person-there tactic. "You make me live by your standards. You're making me be a vegetarian like you. You won't let me have meat in the house."

It didn't work. Alice made one of her snap decisions. "If you want to cook your meat yourself, it's all right with me. Just open the windows because the smell makes me feel sick."

She'd always been firm about the no-meat rule. She'd even objected to my buying hamburger for Rex once he was eating well. Now she changed her mind in half a second. It was very disconcerting.

Alice picked up a pencil. "Now let's get to the housework contract."

All I could think of to say was, "I don't guess everything on the list is absolutely necessary."

⚫━⚫

I told Jill and Melinda. "Would you believe that Alice actually printed up three copies of the contract on the office computer? She gave each of us a copy and put the third one on the refrigerator."

Melinda asked, "Has she stuck to the contract?"

"I figured she'd take about two days to go back to being a total slob. But she turned out to be like Mom about keeping her word."

Jill said, "That's great." She didn't say that she could have told me that Alice would keep her word. Jill was turning out to be a good friend. Sometimes she reminded me a little of Rooji.

I said, "The house is cleaner than I've ever seen it. And I really prefer doing my own laundry. That way my clothes don't come out looking like an elephant sat on them. Even making dinner twice a week isn't that bad. Alice doesn't care if I cook or bring in food as long as she doesn't have to think about it. Also she's out a lot of nights, so I just make myself a ham and swiss cheese sandwich. I'm on a ham and swiss binge."

Jill said, "I guess Alice is out seeing people about the lobbying project."

"I guess so. She doesn't say where she's going." I was embarrassed to admit that it had never occurred to me to ask. Jill was a lot more interested than I was. I told her, "I did hear Alice on the phone talking to Vernon about lobbying. Maybe he's working on it with her. I can't see what good going to Washington will do, but at least it won't land her in court. Not unless she decides to sock our congressman."

Jill ignored my last comment and asked, "Vernon? Isn't he the vet from the Bronx? The guy who came to her trial? Do you think there's romance in the air."

Jill sees romance everywhere. I shook my head. "No. Alice isn't the romantic type."

●━●━●

I reconsidered my answer to Jill a few nights later. Alice was home for dinner, and I'd decided to cook. I made *pasta primavera* (vegetables in sauce over spaghetti) from the *Easy Vegetarian Cookbook* I'd taken out of the library. It came out really good, proving that vegetarian food doesn't have to taste like garbage if you put a little effort into it.

Alice took a second helping and said, "Vernon's animal rights group is having an *a cappella* fund-raising concert Friday night. A cappella is harmony singing without an instrumental backup. Would you like to go with us?"

I knew what a cappella was because we'd sung it in the school chorus. What I didn't know was why Alice was asking me along. Could Jill be on to something? I said cautiously, "I don't know if I want to go all the way to the Bronx."

"The concert's in the East Village, only fifteen minutes by subway. And I know Vernon would like to meet you."

"He already met me. At the trial. Remember?"

"That was only for a minute. You didn't get a chance to get to know him."

Why should I want to get to know Vernon? I hadn't liked the little I'd seen. Could Jill be right? Was there a romance going on? If Alice wanted Vernon and me to get together, it might be more than a romance. Alice was thirty-one, but Mom and Dad had gone to the wedding of a teacher in their school who got married at forty. "You're not thinking of marrying him, are you?"

I said it jokingly, like the idea of Vernon moving in on us didn't scare me. She answered in the same light tone, "I'm not the marrying kind. I value my freedom too much."

"You're the living-together kind. You lived with the artist who painted that weird picture."

"That experience left me leery of ever living with anyone again. Besides, I have more than myself to consider now."

Did she mean that she might live with him if I liked him? "Can I think about it? I mean, about going to the concert?"

●━●━●

Of course, I went to the concert. I told Jill I was going with an open mind. Life with Alice was hard enough without adding know-it-all Vernon, but I swore that wouldn't color my judgment.

It wasn't my fault that Vernon was even worse than I remembered. I told Jill and Melinda at lunch on Monday, "He's one of those people who lectures at you all the time. He spent half the evening lecturing me about animal rights. You know how I love animals. I'm all for saving the whale and the spotted owl, but Vernon would let a million people die of a horrible disease rather than test a cure on one laboratory animal. I didn't even try to argue with him. As far as Vernon is concerned, there's only one right opinion and that's his. It wouldn't be so bad if he was just hipped on animal rights, but he's that way about everything."

Melinda asked, "What did you tell Alice when she asked what you thought of him?"

"She didn't ask."

Jill said, "She probably didn't want to put you on the spot."

"Alice enjoys putting people on the spot; she calls it 'honesty.'"

Jill said, "Maybe Alice isn't serious about Vernon. Maybe

she asked you to the concert because it was a fund-raiser and she had to buy extra tickets."

I shook my head. "Alice distinctly said that she wanted me to get to know Vernon. And she gave me a joking answer when I asked if she was planning on living with him. I know something's going on."

Melinda suggested I watch Alice and Vernon for signs of electricity between them. I said I wouldn't recognize electricity if I fell over it. Jill suggested I have a real talk with Alice. I said I wasn't the real-talk type. It was good to be able to discuss the problem with them, but we didn't come up with any answers. Jill finally said, "Sometimes you just have to wait and see what happens."

●━●━●

Maybe Jill could wait and see. I couldn't. When I ran into Brian while I was walking Rex late that afternoon, I poured out the whole story to him.

He gave me a smart-alecky grin. "Aside from that, Mrs. Lincoln, how was the show?"

When Brian gets like that, the only answer is to go him one better. I said airily, "The concert was nice. There was some medieval and baroque music, but mostly renaissance part singing. You know" —I was sure he didn't know— "Elizabethan *madrigals*."

"That must've been right up your alley. Did your actress friend what's-her-name sing?"

I certainly wasn't going to tell him about my parting from Rooji when he was in this mood. I turned and stalked away. I got as far as the end of Rex's leash. Rex stood firm, sniffing Brian's pockets. I yanked furiously on the leash.

Brian said, "Hey, I was just kidding. What are you so riled up about? You don't still believe you can go back to the past, do you?"

I said, "You're a turd." I was too angry to care that Mom had disapproved of such language. At the moment, Alice was a better model. I treated Brian to her nastiest words and added a few of Ned's curses.

Brian laughed, "A pox on me? Where'd you get that from? Rooji?"

"I thought you didn't remember her name. I thought you didn't believe she existed."

He shrugged. "I only believe in her every other Tuesday."

"You mean you're so wishy-washy you can't stick to a point of view."

"I mean I'm not terrified if I don't have everything in a neat package tied with a bow."

"You'd rather have total confusion." But my heart wasn't in the argument. In his obnoxious way, Brian was saying what Jill had said nicely: You have to go with the flow. How could I let loose when Mom had taught me: A place for everything and everything in its place?

It annoyed me every time she said it.

Where had that disloyal thought come from? If I wasn't like Mom, I'd end up like Alice.

Or would I?

I said, "It's nearly dinnertime. I have to go."

chapter
24

I t was Alice's turn to cook. She was making chili. When I showed her the cookbook I got from the library, she said she didn't have patience with recipes. She'd rather just cook as the mood took her.

The chili didn't come out bad—considering. We were just finishing it when FedEx rang the bell with a package for me. I pried the package open and held up a pair of silver and turquoise Navajo earrings. "Aren't they gorgeous? They're a birthday present from Grandma. The card says she sent them early to make sure I had them in time to wear at my birthday celebration."

Alice looked embarrassed. "When is your birthday?"

"The twelfth."

"Do you want to do something special to celebrate?"

"Mom and Dad always took me to the theater."

She jumped up and came back with the *Times.* "I've never celebrated birthdays, but it's not too late to learn." She opened the newspaper to the theater section, dragging a corner through the remains of her chili. "The British Shakespeare Company is at Lincoln Center. Since you've been studying Shakespeare in school, you might like to see one of his plays performed. They're doing *Romeo and Juliet* for the Saturday matinee on the twelfth. Or would you rather go to a musical?"

"*Romeo and Juliet* would be great."

"I'll go call for tickets."

She came back a minute later with the phone in her

hand. "I just had an idea. You always went to the theater with both your parents. Should I invite Vernon as a stand-in?"

"No!" I hadn't meant to yell. She was trying to do things right. It wasn't her fault that she didn't know how. "What I'd really like is a theater party. With Jill, Melinda, and maybe Kelly. And I'd never hear the end of it if I left Brian out."

"Fine. A theater party it is. I'll order five tickets."

"Five?"

She counted on her fingers, "Jill, Melinda, Kelly, Brian, and you."

"Aren't you coming?"

"If you have your friends, you don't need me."

I didn't need Alice to chaperone. Or to play the hero with Jill or encourage Brian's obnoxiousness. Why did her refusal bother me? I asked, "Don't you like Shakespeare? You took me to Stratford in England." After living with her for seven long months, I knew surprising little about what she really liked. I'd been concentrating on her bad habits.

She said, "I can go with Erica. Maybe we'll catch *Antony and Cleopatra.* I've never seen that performed."

"I thought you wanted to learn to celebrate birthdays."

"My birthday is in February. I'll start then."

Then I caught on. "You're just getting even with me. Showing me how it feels when I stonewall you."

She cleared her throat. "I wouldn't think of competing with you at such games. You'd win hands down anytime. I simply didn't want to be in the way."

I had two choices: to be ashamed or to be angry. Angry was easier. "Don't start that I-don't-want-to-interfere stuff! You only make a big deal of respecting my private space so I won't interfere in *your* life. I can't even find out whether Vernon's going to be around night and day telling us how to live like his way is the only way."

Alice started to laugh. "It's hard to imagine *you* being bothered by *Vernon's* self-righteousness."

"That's not funny! You're just trying to keep me from making a fuss about Vernon moving in on us."

She sobered immediately. "Where did you get the idea that he's moving in?"

"You made me think . . ."

She cut in firmly, "I did not make you think anything. I am not responsible for the fantasies about me you build in your head. I thought I made it clear that I wasn't considering living with Vernon or anyone else right now. If you didn't understand me, it was up to you to pursue the subject. I'm not a mind reader and I'm tired of trying to be one. From now on, if you have a question or a complaint, I expect you to speak up. Am I making myself clear now?"

I muttered, "It's clear," and stared at the beans drying on my plate. A few weeks ago, I'd have retreated into sulky silence. Now the words burst out of me, "I hate Vernon. I don't care what you or Brian or anyone else says. I'm not like him. I'm not!" Even though I was leaving myself open to being clobbered, I couldn't help adding, "Am I?"

Alice didn't clobber me. Neither did she spare me. "Like Vernon, you have strong views about what is right and what is wrong. That can be a great strength or it can make you closed-minded and intolerant of other points of view."

I hit back. "You should talk. When you were ready to go to jail for what you thought was right, how much did you care about my point of view?"

"Maybe we're more alike than either of us wants to admit. Perhaps that's not so surprising since we had the same mother."

She was always coming up with something weird, but this was a record even for her. I demanded, "How could we possibly have the same mother?"

Seeming surprised that I didn't understand what she meant, she explained, "I was only seven when my own mother died. My sister—your mother—was eighteen. She took responsibility for me and pretty much brought me up."

"Why didn't Mom ever tell me that?"

"Maybe she thought she didn't do a good job with me because I didn't turn out more like her. By the time I was your age, everything she did brought out the rebel in me. If she wore a skirt, I wore jeans. If she celebrated birthdays, I ignored them. If she was neat, I was sloppy. If she weighed decisions carefully, I made them in a flash."

That sounded like Alice. No wonder Mom was always annoyed at her. I asked, "Why did you rebel? Was it because Mom was so good at everything that she made you feel like you'd never measure up?"

"I see you know the feeling."

"I don't! Mom never made me feel like that."

She didn't say, "Oh yeah?" She didn't have to. It was written all over her face.

I said, "Anyway, it's better to try to be like Mom than to act the complete opposite."

"It's better to be yourself. It's just harder."

I said, "I don't see what any of this has to do with your coming to my theater party."

Alice let me change the subject. "I thought you didn't want me."

I crowed, "You *thought*! After that lecture you gave me about imagining stuff about you."

She held up her hands in a gesture of surrender. "Got me."

"Well, are you coming or not?"

"I'd enjoy celebrating your birthday with you. It would make me feel like we're becoming a family. But I really understand if you only want your friends."

She was giving me the perfect out. I didn't take it. I said,

"I'd like you to come, only . . ." I finished with a rush. "Only you have to act like a grown-up. You can't do anything weird."

"I'll be a proper and dignified maiden aunt."

"Fat chance!"

chapter
25

S ince Alice had no experience in celebrating birthdays, she just bought theater tickets, said we'd go to dinner afterward, and forgot about it. I had to do all the organizing: ask the guests, pick the restaurant, and arrange when and where to meet.

Jill and Melinda each knew a great restaurant at Lincoln Center. Unfortunately, it wasn't the same one. Jill argued for the Italian restaurant while Melinda insisted the Viennese Cafe had the best cake in town. When I decided on Italian because Alice didn't eat sweets, Melinda said she'd probably have to skip dinner anyway because her cousin's wedding was that night. I said we'd do lunch instead. Jill said of course we would, even though dinner was more festive. Kelly said lunch or dinner was the same to her, but why couldn't we go to a musical instead of a Shakespeare play. Brian didn't object to the play or restaurant. His complaint was he'd be out of place with a bunch of females.

The actors in the Duke's Men always said a bad rehearsal meant a good performance. After the frustrations of planning it, the theater party turned out terrific. I wore my Navajo earrings, and the girls all admired them. The weather was perfect: bright and sunny and not too cold. The restaurant windows framed a view of the plaza where the sunshine turned the dancing fountain waters to diamond drops. A table near the window emptied as the *maître d'* (head waiter) led us toward the back. Alice stopped at the window table saying we'd rather sit there. When he gave her an excuse, she sat down in the nearest chair and waved us into the others. That left him two choices: drag us away or hand us menus.

As we opened our menus, Brian said, "That was a cool move. Did you see the expression on that guy's face when he wished us *Bon appétit*?"

What Brian called "cool," Mom would label "pushy." But it was hard to disapprove when we had the best table in the restaurant. I said, "The rule is: First come, first served. We were here first."

Alice asked, "Does everyone want the complete lunch? It comes with choices of appetizer, entrée, dessert, and beverage."

The complete lunch was $18.75 plus tax and tip. Multiply that by six and add the cost of the tickets and it came to a small fortune. When Alice did something, she went whole hog. I made up my mind to show her that I appreciated it.

The funny thing about looking to praise somebody is that you notice things that usually go right past you. I noticed that when Jill asked, Alice explained that *penne* was a kind of pasta, but she let Jill dither as long as she wanted between that and the *frittata* (a sort of omelet). When Brian started showing off the way boys do around girls and we giggled to encourage him the way girls do with boys, Alice just ate her *minestrone* (vegetable soup). For the first time I understood what she meant by giving people their own space, but that wasn't the kind of thing I could compliment her on. I said the food was great.

After lunch, we did the tourist bit. We gaped at the stories-high Chagall murals in the Metropolitan Opera House, watched a mime perform in the plaza, and poked around the performing arts shop. Then we entered the Vivian Beaumont Theatre. We followed the usher's directions to our seats in the middle of the eighth row of the orchestra, and I forgot about everything else.

The theater was very modern and elegant. It was a long

way from the little playhouse with the open roof where the Duke's Men performed. Yet there was the same excitement in the air, the same feeling of something wonderful waiting in the wings. I gave myself over to the feeling.

The houselights dimmed. The audience quieted, coughed a little, and fell silent. There were a few moments of hushed darkness. Then the stage lights came on to reveal Verona as Will Shakespeare must have imagined it. The chorus, in costumes that put Master Fletcher's satins and velvets to shame, recited a prologue about "star-crossed lovers." A young actress in the chorus looked familiar. Maybe I'd seen her on TV, but I didn't remember what program. By the time I got another glimpse of her in the crowded ball scene, I was too caught up in the play to try to place her.

The plot is kind of silly. Romeo's and Juliet's families are deadly enemies. The two meet at a masked ball, fall in love, and are secretly married by Friar Laurence. When Romeo kills Juliet's cousin in a duel, he is banished from Verona. Juliet's parents—not knowing she is married to Romeo— insist she marry a kinsman. Friar Laurence gives Juliet a drug to make her seem dead. He plans to send for Romeo to rescue her after she is placed in the family tomb, but things go terribly wrong. Romeo, believing Juliet is really dead, drinks poison in her tomb. When Juliet wakes and sees his body, she stabs herself. Only then do their families make up.

Shakespeare turned this plot into magic. The poetry of the language, the romantic love, and the final tragedy were the way life would be if we lived in our imaginations. My heart pounded when Romeo declared his love under Juliet's balcony. I held my breath during the duels and prayed for a happy ending. I cried during the death scenes. When the final curtain came down, I felt I was losing something special and valuable. I tried to hold on to it, but it slipped through my clutching fingers.

The actors took their curtain calls. The bit players stood back while the important actors took their bows. When

Romeo and Juliet came out hand in hand, I clapped until my palms stung. Finally the whole cast linked arms and stepped to the front of the stage. I got a clear look at the actress who had seemed familiar. My hands stopped in midair. It couldn't be!

Rooji looked directly at me and gave a little wave. I waved frantically back. She smiled. Then the curtain dropped and the lights came on. The audience headed for the exits.

As we emerged into the plaza, Jill said she'd adored the play. Brian said the love story was sappy although the duels were great. Melinda said she wished she had a dress like Juliet's to wear to her cousin's wedding. Their voices seemed to come from far away.

Alice said, "Lisa, you're so quiet. Are you all right?"

"I . . . I'm still back in the theater."

Alice smiled. "I knew you'd like *Romeo and Juliet*. You're really a romantic behind that nothing-touches-me pose."

I glared at her. If wishing the world was different made me a romantic, then I was. But that nothing-touches-me crack was totally uncalled-for.

She realized she'd said the wrong thing. Instead of plunging on like a runaway truck racing down a hill, she said, "Everyone should be romantic at your age. Did you know Juliet was only fourteen?" She was learning. Not as fast as I wanted her to, but definitely learning. I guess I was too.

As we passed the Viennese Cafe, Melinda looked longingly in the window. Alice said she could use a cup of herbal tea if the rest of us had our mouths set for sweets. She didn't have to ask twice.

As we polished off our *Sacher torte* (chocolate apricot cake), Jill, who was sitting across the table from me, asked, "Who were you waving at during the curtain calls?" She raised her voice to catch my attention. She caught everyone else's as well.

"One of the actresses in the chorus."

My casual tone didn't fool Jill. She smelled gossip. "How do you know her? The company is from England."

I declared recklessly, "I met her when I was in England. In the Shakespeare garden in Stratford-upon-Avon."

Jill was full of questions. "Was she acting in Stratford? Did she tell you she was coming to New York? Is that why you picked this play?"

I caught Brian looking at me with a let's-see-you-get-yourself-out-of-this expression. To show him, I answered, "She wasn't an actress then, though she was desperate to be one. She said she was going to London to join a theater company."

Melinda asked, "Why didn't you let her know you were in the audience? I'll bet she'd have invited us backstage."

"I didn't see her until the bows. And I'm not certain it was her. Everything looks different in the theater."

Brian said, "Maybe it was *all* your imagination."

I knew what he meant. I insisted, "It wasn't my imagination." Maybe the magic of the play had tricked me into thinking that Rooji had come to bid me a final farewell, but no power on earth would make me believe that she had never existed.

Brian shrugged. "Have it your way."

"I will!"

Alice looked at us curiously, but she didn't interfere. She just said, "I'd better get the check or Melinda will be late for her cousin's wedding."

When everyone said what a great time they'd had, I realized I hadn't gotten around to thanking Alice properly. I tapped my cup with my spoon for attention. Then I didn't know what to say.

I tried, "Thank you all for coming. Especially thank you Alice for buying the tickets and lunch and everything. Also for not making us mind our manners." Somehow that didn't seem to cover it, so I added, "It's the best birthday I ever had."

When I realized what I'd just said, I was horrified. My eyes filled with tears. "I mean, Mom and Dad aren't here, so this can't be the best, but . . ." I was too confused to go on.

Brian rescued me with, "Three cheers for Alice. Hip, hip . . ." It's strange how he can suddenly stop being obnoxious and do exactly the right thing. I guess people aren't all of a piece.

I joined my friends' "Hooray!"

"Hip, hip . . ."

"Hooray!"

"Hip, hip . . ."

We all shouted, "HOORAY!"

Everyone in the cafe was looking at us. That didn't bother Alice one bit. She grinned and said, "My pleasure."

Now that the moment had passed, I knew what I'd really wanted to tell Alice. I'd wanted to say, "Some things you do are great and others are horrible. Sometimes I'm angry at you and sometimes I admire you. And that's how I felt about Mom and Dad, too." That was the important part: that I'd loved my parents and missed them terribly, but they weren't perfect any more than Alice was.

I promised myself I'd remember that the next time Alice did something weird to upset me. I wasn't sure I could keep my promise, but I'd try. Mom and Dad would want me to.

DATE DUE

MAY 14 2002

DATE DUE
